A SLIP OF MURDER

A SEABREEZE BOOKSHOP COZY MYSTERY BOOK 10

PENNY BROOKE

CHAPTER ONE

*P*lease, I told myself, let them not be running behind at the doctor's. I had online orders to pack up. I had calls to return. Plus, I had to prepare for my first-ever guest appearance on a podcast, and I was a little nervous. The host wanted me to comment on the must-read books for summer, and I already had in mind some fun and unexpected titles. I tried some lines out in my head as I hurried through the parking lot and made my way down the sidewalk. I was hoping I could sound insightful with just a touch of wit —but that would only come with practice.

Since I'd focused more on the online presence of the Seabreeze Bookshop, both my business and blood pressure had shot up through the roof. Plus, with the growing list of tasks, my energy was gone. So, despite my busy schedule, I could no longer put off another visit to Dr. Lester Holmes, who would gently reprimand me to fill my fridge up with more veggies and to get more exercise.

Which I, of course, would gladly do if he could magically produce one more hour in my day.

Unfinished tasks jostled for attention in my brain as I headed into the stuck-in-the-nineties waiting room with its orange vinyl chairs and its coffee tables made of cheap veneer. To make my day even worse, Constance Asher, of all people, arrived at the reception desk at the same time I approached. As she always did, the head of the downtown merchants guild looked like she had swallowed a pickled pepper that had sat in the jar too long. Something always seemed to be irritating Constance, a tall, imposing figure with a few frizzy strands escaping from her silver helmet of a hairdo.

"Three-thirty with Dr. Holmes," I told the receptionist—just as Constance spoke *the exact same words* in the precise and throaty voice that had grated on most of the merchants here in town since her term as the head of the guild began about a year ago.

Behind the reception desk, Delilah Bradenton tried unsuccessfully to suppress a girlish giggle. "Whoopsies!" cried Delilah, bringing a wrinkled hand up to her mouth. "Whatever was I thinking when I wrote down

4

those times for today?" She brushed a crumb from the yellow floral dress that strained against her plus-sized figure. Then she turned to us with a heavily lipsticked smile; Delilah's lips today were a vibrant orange. "Why don't we call this little mix-up a blessing in disguise?" She clasped her hands in delight. "Because now you ladies have a chance for a little visit with each other while the doctor's in with Betty Harrell." She lowered her voice to a whisper. "You know, that knee of Betty's still will not behave."

Constance fixed her with a stare. "Some of us, Delilah, do not have time for visits. Some of us have things to do, obligations to fulfill." Her beady eyes grew hard. "And might I suggest that you do the same—with the care and attention the clients in this office should be able to expect."

When Delilah looked to be near tears, I jumped in to speak up. "She mixed up the schedule, Constance. She didn't start a fire or cause something to explode. Delilah, it's just fine."

I was, truth be told, a little irritated myself at Delilah. My to-do list was now looking more like wishful thinking. But the stream of venom coming out of Constance had been way too much. Delilah was...well, Delilah was the worst at taking messages and keeping records, but she went out of her way for clients when it came to other things. Patients, for example, might be surprised with little gifts when they checked out after their appointments. Inspirational paperbacks for those who were struggling with hard news. Or a Tupperware container full of brownies—gluten-free, delicious, and homemade—for those who'd been told that other treats were now off limits.

"Thank you, Rue," Delilah whispered as she stared, confused, at her computer screen. "I don't know how it happened."

Constance, unfortunately, wasn't through. "This is not the first time your incompetence, Delilah, has affected other people. Which is why I brought you this." She reached into a black insulated bag and plopped down a disposable plastic tumbler with the brightest purple shake I had ever seen. "It's called Berry Blast," she said, "and I drink it every day to boost my memory and focus. When I picked up one for myself this morning, I thought it would behoove us all if I brought one along for you." She glared at her victim. "Now, you drink up, Delilah, before one of your mistakes sends a patient to the grave."

Then we heard a deep voice coming from behind Delilah. "A bad attitude and stress will kill you faster, Constance, than any clerical mistake."

I looked up to see Lester Holmes, who had been my

physician since I moved to Massachusetts to take over my gran's store. "Delilah is a valued member of the team," he said. "And while we apologize profusely for the error, I will not allow a member of my staff to be verbally abused." A roundish man with a full head of gray hair, he spoke in the weary voice of a doctor near retirement age who had seen tragedies far worse than double-booked appointments. "Now, Rue, you can follow me to an exam room. And, Constance, I promise to be with you very shortly."

Ha! The childish part of me felt a wave of relief. I'd get seen before Constance and could get on with my day. Perhaps the doctor knew that the longer he kept Constance waiting, the less time she would have to make some merchant feel like dirt when he or she refused to sign on for some silly project Constance had dreamed up. Not that we didn't want to do our part to keep our downtown vibrant, but some of her ideas were over-the-top obsessive. How absurd it would have been, for instance, to compel us all to put yellow pansies only in our outside pots "for a uniform appearance throughout the downtown streets." That would have benefited no one except the local florist—who, not coincidentally, was Constance.

"Sorry for the drama," said the doctor, leading me

into an exam room. He pulled up my chart on a computer and settled his reading glasses on his nose.

"Well, who doesn't make mistakes?" I said.

Lester looked up from the chart and grew thoughtful for a moment. "Constance Asher's manners could stand to be improved," he said. "But I have to tell you, Rue, that a lot of patients echo her concerns—although more politely." He rubbed at his forehead. "Delilah, I'm afraid, grows more forgetful by the day, and it's begun to cause some patients to pull out and ask that their records get sent elsewhere."

"Oh, Lester. I'm so sorry."

He ran a hand through his thick hair. "People stay so busy now. They no longer have the patience to come in for an appointment when I've been called away in an emergency—and no one even bothered to pick up the phone and let them know. And then there are the ones who call in with urgent messages that disappear into... well, who knows where those things go if they're even written down."

"Oh, that does sound bad."

He turned to a cart, grabbed a blood-pressure cuff, and tightened it around my arm. "Well, that's why my own blood pressure is way up," he told me. "But I believe that you're the patient. So let's take a look at what's happening with you." He inflated the cuff slowly and then frowned. "Rue, this isn't good," he announced at last. "If these numbers don't improve, we'll have to try some kind of medication, and I prefer that we avoid that if we can."

"Yes, it was high at home as well. Which is what brought me in."

The success of the new website meant that orders were now coming in from all across the country. It had brought me invitations to speak at conferences and to write guest posts for prominent websites. We'd brought in one extra staffer, but things had begun to happen at a rapid pace, and it was stressful to keep up.

Not that I wasn't grateful. I was excited, blessed—and tired.

Lester listened to my heart and checked my vitals. "Less fat and less sugar? Like we talked about last time?" he asked.

"Given the fact that some of the best restaurants on the planet are within walking distance from my store, I've done okay, I guess." Tourists liked to flock to our sea-kissed paradise, and the to-die-for seafood kept Somerset Harbor on the map. I'd said no that week to garlic butter shrimp at the Lighthouse Kitchen, but when the smell of lobster bisque wafted into the bookstore all day long from the bistro down the street, I could not resist.

"Exercise?" asked Lester.

I knew that one was coming too.

"I used to walk out on the beach several times a week," I told him. "But lately, to be honest, there hasn't been the time."

"You need to find the time." He lifted an eyebrow at me that meant business. "Get more help at the store if you have to, Rue. But I am going to need you to get out on the beach."

"Gatsby would agree." My golden retriever had now taken to sitting down beside his leash and giving me the most persuasive sad eyes he could muster.

"Well, at least I got your buddy Andy to take some time for *himself* and go on a vacation," Lester said. "First one in ten years."

"Fishing in Montana! That has always been his dream." Andy was an investigator *and* a workaholic. His long hours lately had begun to take a toll in sleepless nights and headaches, and this was a vacation that was long overdue.

Lester gave me a small smile. "Half my job is diagnosing and prescribing, and half my job is begging people to be good to their bodies. Fruits and vegetables, exercise and rest. As much as science has advanced, the best cure remains the same—nature's remedy, as old as time."

"Guilty as charged," I said.

He gave me some handouts on ways to lower stress and eat right, and he made me promise to come back in a month.

"Will do," I said, lowering myself from the table. "I should get back to the store so you can call in Constance before she blows a gasket."

As I made my way into the waiting room, the patient in question was still there, scowling in one corner while in another portion of the room, a toddler began to wail. The young mother frowned apologetically as she bounced the girl on her knee and whispered in her ear.

The cries seemed to pull Delilah up out of her seat and across the room. "Oooh, I'll bet she'd love a little story about some very special friends in a big red barn," Delilah cooed. She sat down beside the child and began to read in a soothing voice complete with moos and clucks. That seemed to irk Constance even more, but the young girl was entranced.

"How do you do that?" the mother asked, wide-eyed. "I can never get her to be still for even half a second."

Delilah read some more, the child continued to be quiet, and the phone rang unanswered. But Delilah, I supposed, had talents that did not involve a pen and a message pad.

.   .   .

All of the next week, I took Lester's words to heart as much as my schedule would allow. I was standing at the front desk, munching on carrot sticks and closing up, when Andy made his way into the store. It was a Friday evening; we were closing in five minutes.

"Want to walk with me and Gatsby after I lock up?" I asked him with a smile as I went to dim the lights. "We need to get you, my friend, in tip-top shape for your big trip next week." He had, unfortunately, the stamina and physique of a man who sat more than he moved.

"Well, the trip has been delayed," said Andy with a sigh.

"Andy, no!" I said.

"There has been…a situation, and the chief has let us know he wants all hands on deck." Andy had long ago quit the police force to work in private investigations, but the chief still depended on him when something big was up; none of the detectives were half as smart as Andy.

"What kind of situation?" My heart broke for my friend. For the past month or so, his arms had been in constant motion as he threw out an imaginary bait and hook, a slow grin forming on his face.

Now his face was dour. "I've got some hard news, Rue, and it's about Delilah. Lester found her, I'm afraid, slumped over at the desk earlier today when he was locking up." Andy stuffed his hands into his pockets.

A chill ran through my chest at the words *hard news.* "Does that mean Delilah's…gone?"

Andy rubbed his forehead and gave me a small nod. "And it's looking like the death might have been…" He paused to clear his throat. "It's looking like Delilah was murdered, Rue."

I almost choked on my carrot stick, and I swallowed hard. "But I just saw her last week, Andy!" As if that should have somehow magically kept her safe.

Andy explained that it was Lester who first recognized what could be signs of poisoning, like a tightening of the jaws. Officials were now waiting for the coroner's report, but the death was being treated as a likely homicide.

We were silent for a moment as I absorbed the shock. And then I was filled with rage along with a surge of other dark emotions. "I could use that walk," I said, moving from the counter to the spot where I hung Gatsby's leash.

The dog gleefully ran toward me at the sound of "walk," one of his favorite words.

"I might as well come too," said Andy with a sigh. "Doctor's orders, don't you know."

After I locked up, we headed to the beach, a quick

stroll from the Seabreeze. Both of us were quiet, lost in our own thoughts as we made our way down the beach path and then to the shore. As we walked close enough to let the tide rush almost to our feet, I thought about the last time I had seen my effervescent friend.

The theory of the poisoning had to be off-base. Who could hate Delilah?

Then my mind zoomed to Constance, who had been so furious that day with Delilah.

And she'd brought her a shake.

Which she had bought *before* the inciting incident—but her anger went way back. *This is not the first time your incompetence, Delilah, has affected other people.*

Still, that was crazy thinking. Everyone who came into the office had been frustrated at one time or another over a Delilah mix-up. (And patients' resentment had apparently been at a high, according to the doctor.)

And Constance had been far from the only one to show up at the office bearing food or drink. The ladies of Somerset Harbor were always bringing homemade treats to Lester—and by extension Lester's staff. The beloved doctor was a longtime bachelor, and the women here, especially the widows and the single ladies, took it as their duty to keep the man well fed.

"Any clue," I asked, "on where the poison might have come from?"

"First order of business," Andy said, "is to create a list of those she had recently dined out with—or who might have brought in something for her to ingest."

The list would be a long one.

"This one has hit me hard." Andy paused to stare at the setting sun. "Back when Lester first started in on me to reduce my stress, I told Delilah what was up. And do you know what she would do? She'd email me a little joke first thing every morning." A grin tugged at his mouth. "Corniest jokes you ever heard, which made it even better."

I threw a piece of driftwood, sending Gatsby flying. "Oh, poor Lester," I told Andy. "Today he lost the heart of that little office on the corner."

Andy cleared his throat. "Some would say that Lester has lost much more than that."

That stopped me in my tracks. "What do you mean by that?"

"There are some indications it was...*personal* between him and Delilah."

"As in a romance?" In a lot of ways, they were clearly opposites.

No-nonsense, quiet Lester, who seemed to only own three well-worn Oxford shirts in three pastel shades.

Who preferred to keep to himself despite constant invitations to go out, to come over for spaghetti, to join this club or that.

And bubbly Delilah, who was simply *everywhere.*

But love and logic, I supposed, didn't always go together. In the popular romances that flew off the shelves, they almost never did—in the beginning anyway.

Oh, poor Lester indeed.

For the second time that day, my heart broke in two.

CHAPTER TWO

*S*tacey Carrington slapped another label on a package. "This pretty little bundle will be traveling to Ohio," she told me with a smile, stacking the package on a neat pile of outgoing mail. "I've counted five different states this morning we'll be shipping to."

With online orders up, I had recently hired Stacey to help pack up the books and send them on their way. And I was also glad to have her jump in to assist when the registers got busy.

"Good for you," she told me. "Spreading the love of books from one coast to the next!" I could almost feel the energy bouncing off her wiry frame as she picked up the next book and began to wrap it in what appeared to be a single move.

A woman with Stacey's schedule had to be efficient, I

supposed. While raising three kids on her own, she worked ten hours for me every week while also cleaning a long list of businesses in town.

We worked quietly for a minute while the smallest of my two cats peeped out from a box of outgoing mail.

"Be careful," I teased Ollie as I reached out to scratch his ear. "I don't want the mail carrier to pick up my little buddy and send him off to parts unknown." Then I turned to Stacey. "Who's on your schedule for tonight?"

For once, her light brown ponytail stopped bouncing and her arms went still. "Tonight I clean for Dr. Holmes," she told me with a sigh, crinkling her freckled nose. "Can you believe it, Rue? That she's really gone? I can't get my head around it."

"And how horrific for poor Lester." I chose my words carefully. "I imagine they were...close."

Stacey was observant; she surely knew the scoop—if there *was* a scoop on Lester and Delilah. But as she grabbed another book, she only nodded.

Stacey was observant...and Stacey was discreet. A kind of cleaner's code of ethics, I imagined.

"This town has lost its most enthusiastic fan," I told her thoughtfully as I pulled a mailing label from a sheet.

For any kind of sales promotion or in-store event, there would be Delilah—the first one in the door and bouncing with excitement. No matter how ridiculous,

Delilah was all in. (Or she would pretend to be for the sake of the planner's feelings.)

A contest to name all the lobsters at the entrance of the Crystal Seafood Palace? Delilah was a fan, although teenage girls would sob in the restroom when their dates would order "Wiggles" (with extra butter please) or pick out "Sally Swimmer" for their dinner.

"And do you know what she did lately that deserves a medal in itself?" asked Stacey in a confidential tone. "She'd gone out to lunch a few times with Constance Asher of all people." Stacey made a face. "Something to do, I believe, with a bingo game? And Constance had supposedly pulled Delilah in to help with that."

"Bingo!" my parrot Zeke screamed from his cage.

"Oh, yeah. It's something new—a bingo game for people who come to shop downtown," I explained to Stacey. Players would be sent from one store to another to look for items on their squares. And hopefully, of course, they'd find a special something they couldn't live without. I had to give Constance credit for a good idea on that one. All I'd had to do to participate was to place a replica of Harry Potter's wand next to my tea display.

But now some dark questions had been planted in my mind. Constance that day at the office had been so convinced Delilah was inept. So why had she pulled her in to help with Bingo? Was that only an excuse to get her out to lunch, where she could…

But no. I told my mind to hush. It was only my fatigue and stress causing my thoughts to spiral.

"You spent a lot of time at Lester's office," I told Stacey as I reached for some mailing labels. "Do you have any thoughts on who might have hurt Delilah?" Word about the possible poisoning had spread quickly through the town.

"Oh, there were lots of people who got irritated at her when they needed someone to *pick up the phone already* or give a message to the doctor." Stacey smoothed a seam out on a package. "But I can't imagine anyone who would want to see her die. Everyone adored Delilah."

"Does anything stand out from the last few weeks?" I asked. "That she might have said or done?"

"Well, now that you ask…" Stacey paused. "I was almost sure it was only in her head, but now I just don't know."

I waited quietly for her to go on.

"Okay, here's the thing." She let out a long breath. "About a month ago, Delilah started staying late to chat while I cleaned the office—which I didn't mind, of course. She was always so much fun." She gave me a pointed look. "But then I figured out the reason that she did it. She was scared to go back home."

I held back a gasp. "But why?"

Stacey ran her hand through her ponytail and frowned. "Now I feel kind of bad that I just brushed it off. But she swore that she had heard somebody prowling in her yard and brushing up against the windows. And she told me she'd heard footsteps out behind the kitchen porch." She sighed. "And I would try to be supportive, while in my mind I rolled my eyes. You know how Delilah was," she said with a shrug. "Everything was always just a little more dramatic when Delilah told a story. And I just kind of figured that it had to be the wind. Or a squirrel, you know?"

"Well, I would have thought the same," I rushed to reassure her. "And you are right about the drama. She always loved a mystery and could never leave the store without a stack of horror books. Maybe not the best choice for someone who lived alone—and with a big imagination like Delilah."

"But if what they say is true—that she was maybe poisoned?" Stacey leaned across the counter and let out a sigh. "Oh, Rue! What if she was right?"

"Did you tell the cops?" I asked.

"I did," said Stacey softly as her phone interrupted with a buzz. She glanced down to check. It was quite the juggling act, balancing the details of her daily life: making sure there were no new emergencies from her childcare or her children's schools or one of her cleaning clients.

The tinkling of the bell on the door, along with Gatsby's joyful bark, signaled the arrival of a customer, and I looked up to see Reg, the owner of the men's store down the street, make his way into the store. My part-timer Beth was helping other customers, so I stepped out to say hello. "I'll bet you've come in to get the new James Patterson," I told Reg with a smile. The book had just come out that day.

He grinned. "I believe you read my mind! The plot for this one sounds amazing. So I'm afraid the chores around the house this week are gonna have to wait while I disappear and read." He looked down at the carpet and fiddled with his tie. "And to be honest, Rue, the distraction will be welcome. We've all had such a blow." Delilah lived next door to Reg, so I knew the news would have hit him hard.

"Can you believe it, Reg?" I asked him with a sigh. "I've had her on my mind all day. Had she seemed okay to you in the last few weeks?"

"Everything seemed fine." He reached down to pet Gatsby, whose tail was a happy blur. "We had her over to the house last week when I cooked steaks out on the grill. And she was the same as ever—full of stories, making plans to take some kind of painting class at the recreation center. There was always something new on the horizon with Delilah," he said, smiling at me sadly.

I nodded with a frown, my thoughts still stuck on that supposed prowler at Delilah's house. "Reg." I hesitated. "Did she ever mention...hearing someone in her yard?"

He looked up, surprised. "She did!" He sighed and shook his head. "I got those calls a lot. I'm afraid it didn't take a lot to spook Delilah. But I always tried to be a good neighbor to her. So I would go and check—and walk around her place just to reassure her that no one was there." He grew silent for a moment, scrunching up his brow as if he'd remembered something. "But I have to tell you that about ten days ago, she called me kind of late; it was sometime after ten. And this time it felt...different."

A knot hardened in my chest. "It felt different how?"

"Well, she swore up and down she had heard somebody *crying* out there in her yard. And that had never been a thing she had said before." He frowned. "And then there was the pie."

"The pie?"

"She'd left a pie out on the porch—blueberry, I believe. Had herself a little picnic and forgot to bring it in—or to even have a slice. And when I walked around the outside of her house to check, it was the strangest thing: something—or somebody— had taken a big bite. Because there it was, a smushed-in hole in her perfect crust, like some scoundrel out there had been fooling with her pie." Reg frowned, stooping down to rub Gatsby's back. "Now, you'd think they'd *take* the pie if they were on the prowl. Everybody knows there's nothing sweeter than a Delilah pie." He shrugged. "It could have been some animal, I'm thinking. Some raccoon that night might have had a fine dessert. But that—along with the crying that she'd heard—really rattled her."

I took a calming breath and processed what I'd heard.

Was that when it had happened? Had someone slipped some poison into Delilah's perfect pie, hoping she would take a fateful bite later on that night?

CHAPTER THREE

*M*y mind reeled for a moment.

Then it hit me that Reg was talking still. So I took a calming breath and tuned back in to the conversation.

He had also heard the rumor that Delilah had been poisoned. But some of his customers insisted it was stress that had made her heart give out. "It was something personal that was going on between her and a friend; that is what I'm hearing," Reg said thoughtfully.

More than one of his customers that day had come in with that opinion. But no one had any details, only scattered observations to support the rumor. It was said, for instance, that Delilah had skipped church for three weeks in a row—as if she might have wanted to avoid someone. One man had overheard a complaint from her that most decidedly was not a Delilah thing to say. Something about big mouths and little minds and a love for trouble.

"I'm not one for rumors, but I think they might be right about some kind of conflict," Reg said with a frown. "I was working in the yard about two weeks ago, and I heard Delilah in the middle of some kind of argument. She was with some woman, but I could not tell who." He crossed his arms and set his mouth in a thin firm line. "It was unusual for sure, but I didn't think a lot about it until I heard that someone might have hurt her. And now I have to wonder…"

I moved closer to him, my mind on alert. "What was the fight about?"

"I couldn't hear a lot." He put his hands on his hips and cocked his head to the side. "I swear I heard the words *magical bassoon.* Although you don't have to tell me that makes no sense at all."

I thought for a moment. "Surely it was something that *sounded* like bassoon."

"But it came through pretty clear—*bassoon*. It was the only part of the whole conversation I could really hear," he said. "Because right at that moment the wind died down a little, and the neighbor on the other side stopped mowing for a second." Staring at the floor, he shook his head. "If I had known Delilah was about to die

—maybe about to be murdered—I would have looked to see whose car was parked out in the drive."

The rest of the day was busy. It happened to be a Tuesday, when publishers traditionally liked to release new books. A big sale at the boutique next door sent a lot of browsers into my store as well. Not to mention that Somerset Harbor loved to get out and gather when big news came to town.

The day passed in such a rush that I didn't notice until late that Reg had left his book sitting on the counter after he checked out. Hmm. His house was on my way home and I could slip it into his mailbox; I knew how anxious he had been to get going on the read. Plus, it couldn't hurt to walk around in Delilah's yard and take a look around in case someone had really been there—weeping in her yard, messing with the pie, or whatever. What if they'd dropped something and the cops had missed the clue?

And for all I knew, the cops hadn't looked at all. I understood from Andy they were looking mainly at those who'd dined out with Delilah or gone to Lester's office bearing treats. And the local cops were in the habit of choosing just one focus in an investigation, ignoring any clues that hinted that the answer might be found down a different path.

Thank goodness there was Andy, who really knew

his stuff. Because as gorgeous and upscale and friendly as Somerset Harbor was, we had seen far more than our share of murders.

When the workday finally ended, I grabbed my purse and Reg's book and called out for Gatsby, who was napping in the back. "Come on, boy, let's go! Would you like a surprise?"

"Surprise, surprise!" said Zeke.

Gatsby loved the little creek that ran behind Delilah's house, and he was fascinated by the birds that came to the many feeders she'd put up in her gardens.

He perked up at the word "surprise" and let out a happy bark. Hopefully he would not be disappointed that cheese was not involved.

I remembered with a pang my last phone call with Delilah, who had urged me to stop by to pick for myself some of her gorgeous daffodils that were now in bloom. She knew they were my favorite flower. As I put the leash on Gatsby, I decided I would do just that. I could set the cheerful yellow blooms on my desk as a reminder of my friend.

After a short drive, I left the book in Reg's mailbox and parked in Delilah's drive, taking note that someone had driven her Ford Fiesta from the office and parked it by the porch. Something about the well-kept blue car looked sad as it sat there motionless, no more adventures to be had.

I let Gatsby out, and he ran toward two red birds at a feeder, causing them to scatter. I smiled at the dog, glad to stretch my legs and take in the quiet after a long day. I willed myself to relax as I breathed in the bouquet of scents that rose up on the garden path that led down to the river. How odd that Delilah would not step out onto the porch and give me a happy wave. But the mayflowers and red trilliums that crowded the path with color seemed to say that life went on.

As Gatsby ran ahead, I kept my eye on the ground, noticing a piece of trash, which I promptly grabbed—as Delilah would have wanted. Delilah loved her gardens, lavishing on them the same tender care she'd give to a frightened patient. I looked down at the torn sheet of paper in my hand that contained two words in a neat cursive script: *Crépuscule* and *Ravie.*

I'd ask Google later if the world wide web could make any sense of that.

Then I also noticed what appeared to be several grapefruit peels scattered here and there around the plants. There was a bit of wrapper that had once contained some breath mints. And, now that I looked closely, the soil around the flowers had been loosened, as if someone had been digging, leaving somewhat of a mess.

If the intruder had been real, had he or she been eating grapefruit and picking flowers as they prowled around the yard? What was I missing here?

I was picking a bouquet and pondering when Gatsby suddenly stood still, as if he had spotted something. By that point, he had run past the river to the far portion of the yard, near a thick patch of woods. He stared out into the trees beyond the property and let out a low growl.

"What is it, boy?" I asked as I hurried toward him.

He began to bark as I got there just in time to make out the sound of footsteps behind a grove of balsam firs that divided the yard from the woods. And then I was startled by a flash of hot-pink shoe below a leafy branch. It was a blur of motion, quickly gone. But I managed to make out a sturdy heel, a zipper, and a tassel as a crunch of leaves announced the retreat of the figure further into the woods.

Gatsby's bark grew louder, more protective of the yard that had been so special to his friend.

"Gatsby, it's okay," I said as I knelt down to soothe my buddy.

There was no need, you see, to sneak into the woods to try to solve the mystery.

Because I recognized those boots.

CHAPTER FOUR

I could not move for a moment because I was too stunned. *Why was Judy Harrington running behind Delilah's yard?*

What I had just witnessed was too crazy to believe.

What the heck was going on?

I knew Judy fairly well, stopping often at her place, Whiskers and Coffee Beans, three blocks from the Seabreeze. Since the café had opened earlier that year, patrons loved the chance to sip on specialty lattes and other drinks while cuddling with and being entertained by the cats in residence. Judy usually had about nine or ten, all strays she had brought in for customers to meet and adopt.

She once had filled me in that while a coffee drinker might *think* he or she was the one to choose a cat, the cats themselves most often did the choosing. I had witnessed it myself. I was there one day when a tiny calico snuggled into the ample lap of Otto Greene, who had been dragged into the café by his long-suffering wife. Most of us had Otto pegged as a rude bank teller who we tried to avoid as much as possible. But not the little cat, who promptly fell asleep against Otto's crisp white shirt, causing him to coo in a way that was so unlike Otto his wife could only stare.

Judy was a white-haired former hippie who preached "Peace, love, cats and coffee" with a smile as serene as the instrumental music that played in the café. She would slip you a free latte if you were having a bad day. And she was about as far from the killer type as anyone could get.

But there had to be a reason she'd been at Delilah's or close by. And had apparently run into the woods when she heard somebody in the yard.

Had she seen that it was me? I could not be sure.

Judy and Delilah had spent a lot of time together as part of the Vintage Divas, a group of widows and single ladies over sixty-five. The Divas met for drinks and dinner and traveled as a group to gardens and attractions in the towns that surrounded Somerset Harbor. No canasta games and quilting nights for them. Instead, they outlasted everyone in the local dance-athon to raise money for the food bank. They'd been extras in a movie about an alien invasion in a retirement home. And the Diva Dessert Table was the first place I headed toward at any town event. For days after that, I'd dream of creamy custard and gooey butter cake.

Although they all were friends, the competition among the ladies could veer to the extreme. Over who had the best recipe for marinara, whose new cut and color made her look more youthful, and who deserved the solo in the Easter morning service. But the group was mostly close, and if you heard raucous laughter coming from a table when you were out to eat, it was a good bet the Divas were close by.

Still shocked at the idea of Judy as a stalker, I picked my daffodils and pondered. Then I called for Gatsby to get in the car. Because tonight would be a good night to stop by Judy's for a latte. Judy herself was obviously elsewhere at the moment, but maybe she had plans to run back to the café after her...activity for the evening.

Fifteen minutes later I arrived at Whiskers and Coffee Beans. The smells of coffee and cinnamon wafted from the building, a bright blue former private residence at the edge of town. Inside, quiet music mingled with a low chorus of meows, and a black cat nuzzled at my ankle to welcome me to his home.

"Well, hello!" I bent down to stroke the cat's soft fur as Gatsby settled into a corner for a nap. Two gray kittens right away snuggled up against his tummy to join him for the snooze fest.

A tall teenage boy looked up from the counter with a smile. "Welcome to the café," he said. "What can I fix for you today?"

A big ginger-colored cat stood over to the side watching him intently.

"A Cheshire Cat's Caramel Latte Extravaganza, please," I said. "I'd like a medium, and could you make that decaf?" I reached into my purse to pull out my wallet. "Is Judy off tonight?"

"She had to run out for a bit, but she should be back," said the boy. He quickly fixed my drink and handed me a steaming mug. Then he gently picked the cat up for a snuggle.

I found a table near the counter and quietly enjoyed my drink. At almost closing time, the café was fairly empty, except for a large table of high schoolers who sat studying their phones like there might be a test.

Too amped up to let my mind rest, I pulled out the scrap of paper I'd found in Delilah's yard and googled the two words. They were French, it turned out. For "twilight" and "delighted."

The first one, I supposed, might fit into some murder plot: to denote the time of a delivery of poison. Or the time of day Delilah might appear at a certain place to take a fateful bite.

But "delighted"?

No way did that one fit.

I'd been there for about ten minutes when Judy breezed in through a side entrance. The gray bun atop her head looked a bit disheveled, and she seemed out of breath. But not enough so that I would have noticed if I had not just seen her—or her boots at least—running through the woods at a fast clip.

With a smile on her face, she made a beeline for my table. "Rue! How are you doing, dear?"

I gave her a rueful smile. "I guess we've all been better."

"Ah, yes." She let out a sigh as she sank into the chair across from me. "These golden years, they say, are supposed to be the best years—and she deserved to have a whole lot more of them."

"It is just horrific," I agreed. "So hard to comprehend." I took a sip of my latte and tried to keep my voice light as I got to *the* question. "What have you been up to? Did you get to take a bit of time off tonight?"

She seemed to think about her answer, and a sad looked crossed her eyes. "I had to keep a promise," she told me quietly when she spoke at last. "I guess you could call it a favor for a friend."

There was no guilt in her expression, just the kind of deep distress I myself had felt.

I had to keep her talking. And maybe I could get just a little hint about what was up with Judy.

"Have you heard what they are saying?" I picked up my mug. "All the talk, I mean, about Delilah being poisoned?"

"I don't know what to think!" said Judy. "Could that possibly be true?"

A snow-white cat lay its palm on her leg and she scooped it up as she continued talking. "All the Divas have been in to trade theories back and forth and tell our Delilah stories," Judy said then leaned in close. "Poor Patsy Kettles took it hardest out of all of us, I think."

Patsy ran Sophisticated Soaps, a bath and beauty shop downtown.

"Oh, yes! I knew those two were tight," I said.

"Well, they *were* close at one time," confided Judy. "But for the last month or so, there was something up between them. It made things very tense at some of our Diva outings. All of us couldn't help but notice the extremely rude remarks that Patsy directed at Delilah.

Although she never specified what Delilah might have done to put her in such a snit."

"So you have no idea?" I asked.

"Oh, who knows with Patsy." Judy touched her nose to the cat's as she rubbed its back. "Patsy, as you may know, is prone to causing drama," she continued. "She likes to have her way and does not want to be crossed. But I could tell that poor Delilah just had no idea how to react." Judy gave me a look. "Some of us can dish it back to Patsy, but Delilah was too sweet; she didn't play those games."

I guessed a trip to the soap shop was in my future too.

I glanced toward the front, where the employee swept beneath a table as the ginger-colored cat nuzzled at his feet.

"Hey, Ricky," Judy called. "There's some extra food and litter in the back you can take home with you tonight."

He looked up, confused. "But I don't have a cat," he said.

Judy winked at me. "Oh, I believe you do. Butterscotch just picked you out."

The door to Judy's office was ajar, and I could see a dozen pink and yellow roses sitting on her desk.

"Did someone pick *you* out?" I teased. "Might those flowers be from a new man in your life?"

She looked down and blushed. "Well, as you may know, I decided a while back I was through with men," she said in a girlish whisper. "But they always say love takes you by surprise! And guess who I'm having dinner with tomorrow at the Seafood Palace? It is the same fine man who is taking me this weekend to the movies!"

When I didn't answer, she raised a playful brow. "The flowers on my desk came from a certain doctor with whom I've been spending time." Her blush grew even deeper. "I do believe it might be serious between me and Lester. Can you believe it, Rue?"

I thought of Andy's words about the doctor: *There are some indications it was personal between him and Delilah.*

I glanced down nervously at the dirt-flecked boots on Judy's feet, unsure what to think.

"Um, I need to let you go since it's getting time to close." I almost stumbled and knocked my latte over as I stood to go. "Judy, you take care."

CHAPTER FIVE

he next morning, I was still feeling shaken as I watched my best friend line up vintage photos for the new display in her corner of the store. Locals loved the old postcards, letters, and old-fashioned ads she found for her ever-changing, whimsical displays. One never knew what memory—or which ancestor even—one might come across underneath the sign that spelled out in black and silver "Antiquities by Elizabeth."

This month's display was titled "Best Friends Through the Years."

"You okay?" she asked. She frowned at me before setting down a black-and-white photo of two toddlers leaning against what looked to be a 1960s Thunderbird. Next to it she placed a yellowed greeting card on which three baby squirrels were holding up a sign: "Sharing Treasures with Your Friends is Life's Sweetest Joy!" It was a little touch of humor, given the willfulness with which one of the girls was holding on to her Mr. Potato Head. This child, it seemed, had found no joy in the "sharing" as her friend reached to grab the toy.

"You seem tired today," said my own best friend, concern wrinkling her brow. "Shall I get you some tea?"

"Thank you. I'm okay, but this thing with Delilah has hit me pretty hard," I said.

Needing a shot of caffeine, I fixed some tea for us both. Then I sunk down into the floral chair beside her table, and I caught her up, beginning with what had happened in Delilah's yard.

She listened, disbelieving, then let out a gasp when I got to Judy's revelation at the cat café. *"Lester?* With Judy *and* Delilah?" Elizabeth put down the stack of photos she was holding. "That does not sound right to me."

"Well, that is what she said. And I saw the flowers for myself."

Elizabeth gave that some thought. "Women in this town have been chasing Lester since he came to town and set up practice in the eighties," said my friend, who had lived in Somerset Harbor for most of her life. "But I don't believe I've ever known a one who caught him."

"They've been chasing *Lester?* Really?" I took a sip of

tea. I had always loved my doctor for his kindness and good sense, but he hardly seemed the type for women to chase after. Some of the older widows, it was true, loved to fill his fridge with homemade meals, not wanting our hard-working Lester to subsist on frozen dinners. It was a bit of playful flirting, maybe, among the older set, but nothing more than that—or so I had always thought.

Elizabeth noticed my confusion and gave me a shrug. "Maybe it's because he's a single doctor? All I know is that certain women seem to have 'little colds' on a frequent basis, perhaps to have a reason to stop by the office?" She studied a photo and added it to the display. "He might have gone out on a few dates every now and then over the years, but, as far as I can tell, he hasn't shown real interest in any one of them. Lester Holmes is married to his work, or so it seems to me."

The idea made me sad; I would have liked to think that Lester had someone nice to talk to over dinner after he'd spent his whole day listening with care to other people's problems. (And it seemed he might indeed have had more than one someone.)

"Maybe he's the type who likes to keep things private?" I suggested.

"I do see him out sometimes." Elizabeth paused to think. "But never in a situation that seems at all romantic."

Of one thing I was sure. If he ever did decide to give romance a try, it would be unlike Lester to give Judy the idea that things were serious between them if he was seeing someone else as well. Of course, Andy hadn't seemed to know for sure that Delilah and the doctor were a couple. He'd only hinted that it had been implied as the police had gone about their investigation.

But the two of them together made no sense to me. When I'd seen Lester at his office, he had seemed disgruntled by the way Delilah's little slip-ups were causing customers to take their business somewhere else. What I had picked up that day had been frustration, not romantic inclinations toward his receptionist.

Elizabeth sighed and added another photo to the display. This one showed three older women laughing as they sat on a bench surrounded by a sea of shopping bags. Delilah, sweet and open-hearted, must have thought that *she* had friends like that as well. Who would laugh with her in the good times and have her back when things got hard. But had she, in fact, been done in by one of the Vintage Divas?

Was there a darkness among this group of friends I had not suspected? They had always seemed so close. But then there was Judy, sneaking around like some kind of prowler in the yard of her late friend and fleeing through the woods. And what could have been the trouble between Patsy Kettles and Delilah?

"Elizabeth," I asked, "do I recall correctly that you worked with Patsy Kettles a few months ago—after her mother died?"

"I did." Elizabeth shuffled through some papers, interspersing several hand-addressed envelopes among her display of photos. "Her mom saved everything, and I bought a lot of photos, old programs from community events—you know, that type of thing—from the estate. There was quite a lot of stuff that I'm still going through."

"Any trouble that Patsy mentioned between herself and Delilah?"

When Elizabeth answered me with a question in her eye, I explained what I had heard from Judy about Patsy's treatment of Delilah toward the end.

"Interesting," said Elizabeth. "Now that you mention it, she did mention something odd that has stuck with me ever since. I mentioned that I'd seen Delilah when I went into the office about my allergies." She frowned, deep in thought, as she placed a photograph just so.

"And...?" I prompted her when she did not go on.

"And Patsy—it was so surprising—just went on a tirade. She kind of turned her nose up, told me that

Delilah had a lot of people fooled, that Delilah had a side that was greedy, very pushy."

"That's not true at all!" I said. Delilah had her faults, but her heart was pure. I had a lot of faith in myself as a judge of character. To find maximum success in the bookselling world, one must be adept at not only reading books but at reading customers as well. My job, after all, is to match a customer with a world of fiction they'll go on to inhabit for a period of hours. A sort of travel agent who can send them overseas by lunchtime or even across time. But you have to know your customer to know the kinds of worlds they'd like to visit most.

"I could not believe the things I heard coming out of Patsy's mouth." Elizabeth shook her head. "And I said to her, 'Why in the world would you even say a thing like that about Delilah?' But she just mumbled something she seems to have witnessed…I think on a bridge? She clammed up after that."

"So weird."

Elizabeth tied a silk violet bow around a stack of letters, which she placed at the center of the table. Her latest display was set to open the next week. Anyone who spotted themselves in a photo would receive a five-dollar coupon for themselves and one for the friend in the picture too. Plus, they, of course, could buy the photo once the show had closed, and people almost always snapped up anything they spotted with a personal connection.

Elizabeth set out another faded greeting card: "Friends enhance your life."

Could they take it away as well?

Next, I helped a group of teens select some books for a history project, then I texted Andy to tell him we should talk. The day got busy after that, which helped to get my mind somewhat off the murder. There was no escaping it completely, though, since a lot of customers had things to say about Delilah and her untimely end.

When I could, I slipped back to my office to put some thoughts down for the upcoming podcast, but the words wouldn't come. It was hard to keep my mind on 'New and Exciting Fiction' when horrors from the real world were crying to be solved. The pie-tasting prowler, the cryptic notes in French, the odd behavior of the Divas. What could it all mean?

I checked my phone, but no response had come in so far from Andy.

The questions seemed to press into a point just above my eye, and I felt the warning of a headache coming on. I ran my fingers through my hair and leaned back in my chair, letting out a sigh. At least it was my day to get off at four, and I had planned a hot bath with my advanced reader copy of the latest title by Lisa Scottoline. Today I was distracted, but I could count on her most days to grab my attention from page one and not let go. Normally on the days I got off early, I would treat myself to two perfect macarons—pistachio and salted caramel were the ones I craved the most. But I'd do as Lester said, despite the fact that a bubble bath with apple slices sounded way less decadent and fun.

My kindly doctor friend might have a secret life worthy of the more intriguing offerings on my shelves, but he knew his stuff when it came to health. So an apple it would be.

Although…maybe I could treat myself instead to something special at Sophisticated Soaps. Hopefully, Patsy would be working, and she could fix me up.

Andy, of course, would call it "snooping." I could hear him now: "Rue, you should stick to selling books, and let *us* do our jobs."

Well, I wasn't stopping him from his investigation! I was only planning to go shopping and maybe ask some questions while Patsy rung me up. The invigorating scents and the feel of some high-grade lotion on my skin would go a long way to ease my anxiousness—and with any luck, my blood pressure would go down to somewhere near acceptable.

That was what the doctor ordered, and so off I went.

CHAPTER SIX

he interior space of Sophisticated Soaps was designed to soothe as soon as a customer stepped onto the white and beige oriental rug that lay at the front entrance. Soft jazz was playing low, and the scents of lavender and sandalwood rose up to greet me.

"Rue! So good to see you." Patsy Kettles strolled out from behind the desk as if she were competing in Atlantic City rather than selling soaps in our little town. Her hair, a perfect shade of honey blonde, fell to her shoulders in soft curls. Only a few wrinkles around the eyes hinted that she was in the sixty-something club with the other Divas.

"I was ordered by my doctor to relax, and I figured you would have the perfect thing," I told her with a rueful smile.

"Easier said than done after what we've all been through." She shook her head. "But I do believe I can fix you up with a little magic," she told me with a wink. She strode over to the left and took three bars of soap from a shelf, laying them out on the counter. With their gorgeous boxes or foil wrappers, Patsy's products looked more like works of art than something to be used up in a bath or shower. The shiny wraps in many colors picked up the light from scattered candles placed around the store.

"These three are my current favorites," Patsy said in her deep, rich voice. She picked up a white bar with a scroll design in the center showing through its pink clear wrapping. "This one will absolutely take you to another world. Just smell."

I did, breathing in a delicate rose scent. "Oh, yes. That one is divine," I said. In the end, I bought all three, along with some almond-scented lotion, which Patsy packaged for me in a lavender and pink bag with one S intertwined around another.

"This will be perfect. Thank you," I said and touched her hand. "And, Patsy, how are you? I know how close you were to Delilah."

"Oh, Rue. What a shock. And I just can't imagine who would ever hurt Delilah. The two of us were like sisters." Her voice seemed to crack. "In fact, we were supposed to have lunch today, to try out that new café on Third Street."

"Well, it sounds like you stayed close right up to the end. No regrets and all of that, which must be such a comfort," I said. "I've lost people in my own life when we hadn't left things on the best of terms," I added in a voice I hoped would invite any confidence she might want to unburden. "I have to imagine that happens quite a lot with the way that death can take you by surprise. You think that you have time to fix things, and then your friend is gone."

"Oh, yes. We got along so well! I just adored Delilah."

I studied Patsy, whom I knew fairly well from the merchants guild, although she was not a reader. What secrets lay behind those perfectly made-up eyes? Perhaps the deadly kind? Those were, after all, the kinds of secrets one took great care to hide.

Then something caught my eye against the patchwork of color that was the soap display. A vase of yellow and pink roses stood tall on a side counter, the buds having only just now reached their perfect point of bloom.

"Oh, roses!" I exclaimed. "How lovely."

She smiled at me shyly. "I haven't told a lot of people, Rue, but I have a beau. Can you imagine—at my age?"

She lightly touched her hair. "Although I do try my best to keep up my appearance."

"Oh, that's wonderful," I said, although I had an uneasy feeling about who they might be from.

And then Patsy giggled, which Patsy never did. "Lester Holmes, I tell you, is just the sweetest man. And he is taking me this weekend to the movies!"

Which I guess had been scheduled carefully around his dinner date with Judy. What on earth was Lester thinking? If he wasn't careful, this kind of juggling act could make his own blood pressure problems rival mine.

"Oh, yes, Lester is the best," I said once I had caught my breath. "How long has this been going on?"

"Well, we've kept it kind of quiet, but for about six months." She placed a hand over her heart and blushed.

Long enough that her tirade against Delilah could have been inspired by this love triangle. Well, Lester had been too busy to call it a triangle. He apparently had made three women in town giddy, maybe more.

My phone buzzed with a text. "Drinks on the porch tonight?" It was Andy writing back; he loved a good whiskey on the big front porch of my gran's house, which I now called home. I had taken over the bookshop from my gran when she began her retirement, complete with extensive trips and visits to friends across the country.

"Gatsby and I will happily await your arrival," I typed back.

A drink would be welcome, as would time with Andy. I had a lot to tell him about his investigation.

CHAPTER SEVEN

*S*everal hours later, I felt somewhat more relaxed as I sipped a buttery chardonnay out on the porch, my skin still warm and silky from my rose-scented bath.

Gatsby sat eagerly at Andy's feet, studying my friend as if he were a piece of groundbreaking art. Despite the fact that I was the provider of Gatsby's meals, toys, and (admittedly dwindling) walks, Andy had become, almost at first sight, his favorite person in the world.

Tonight, I sensed that was a good thing, that Andy really needed some hero worship from my dog. Always worn down from his work, he seemed especially despondent now as he started in on his second whiskey. His work was hard on Andy, who felt deeply for the victims and also had to navigate a police bureaucracy that often stifled his best instincts on how to catch the crooks. And at the moment I could tell he was thinking of the rainbow trout he would not be catching in the Bighorn River, which he had once described for me as an angler's paradise.

When I asked about the case, I only got a grunt and the usual stream of words about how sensitive information was for official sources only. Blah, blah, blah, blah.

I took another sip. "Well, I myself have come across some tidbits I'd like to pass along to the very grouchy and *official source* in the seat across from me," I began. Anticipating his reaction, I held up a hand. "I wasn't snooping, Andy. I came across this information in the course of picking flowers, buying soap, and sipping coffee. The usual activities of a woman going about her day."

He frowned, not convinced. Then he let out a sigh and threw out an imaginary fishing line. His mind was in Montana and not on my perceived misdeeds. "Okay, Rue, I'm listening. Let me hear what you've got."

I leaned forward in my chair. "Okay, here's the thing. I have to wonder, Andy, if it all had to do with the romance you mentioned earlier between Lester and Delilah." I paused for effect. "Our dear Dr. Holmes, it seems, is quite the ladies' man, and some of the other women might not have been too happy that Delilah had her eyes on him as well." I cocked my head to study Andy. "Were you aware that there were others?"

Andy squinted, staring straight ahead as he reeled in his imaginary fish, which seemed to be a big one. "No, Rue, I was not," he said. "But I hardly think that jealousy over Lester's love life would be any reason for a perpetrator to..." His voice trailed away as he wrestled with the fish. Gatsby's head moved back and forth, following the progress of the imaginary trout.

"I would normally agree," I said, scooping my cat Beasley up into my lap. "But I caught one of his other paramours fleeing through the woods behind Delilah's house when I showed up to pick flowers. Which really made me wonder: was she looking for evidence, perhaps, that she might have left behind when she was there before to stalk Delilah?"

Andy stared at me, wide-eyed.

"And another one of Lester's women had been acting out against Delilah in the weeks before the murder. Or the *presumed* murder, I should say."

"Oh, no. It's now officially a murder; the poisoning has been confirmed," said Andy. The shock of my news had apparently knocked all the "private-information" nonsense from his mind. Plus, Andy was aware that I could be discreet.

"But Rue, who and what...?" he stammered.

But I was on a roll, eager to get out all the information before I answered questions. "Are the police aware that in the weeks before the murder someone was apparently trespassing in Delilah's yard?"

"We are indeed aware of those reports. But we are aware as well it was our victim's habit to assume the worst when it was just the wind or acorns falling on the roof."

"But I've never known an acorn or a breeze that could take a bite out of a blueberry pie," I said as Andy's eyes grew wide. "Delilah," I explained, "had left it on the porch the night she heard the noises." I rubbed behind Beasley's ear. "This time when she heard 'footsteps,' I think it was really footsteps that Delilah heard."

"Interesting," mused Andy. "And how on earth did you...?"

I picked my glass up from the table. I wasn't finished yet. "Oh! And some intruder—the one with the sweet tooth maybe—left behind a note. Which spoke romantically of moonlight and delight."

"This note spoke of *what?*"

I pulled the paper from my pocket and handed it to him. "It's in French, by the way." I paused for a breath. "And I also figured out that someone had been messing with Delilah's garden just before her death," I continued. "That made quite a disarray of the mayflowers that she loved. And as a little hint, it was someone who loved grapefruit! Maybe that will help."

Andy squinted his eyes in confusion.

"Also, were you aware a loud argument took place in Delilah's yard about two weeks ago? I believe it was regarding a magical bassoon, which I know makes no sense."

"I have so many questions I think I might explode." Andy shook his head.

So I sat back in my rocking chair and gave him all the details.

After I was finished, he took a slow sip of whiskey. "Well, that is very helpful, Rue," he said, "regarding Judy and Patsy, who have not been on our radar. We've had our eye instead on another suspect as the likely source of the poison that Delilah drank."

Drank, he said. Not *ate*. My mind went to Constance, handing over that neon purple drink, fury radiating from her eyes.

Andy almost instantly recognized his slip. "I didn't say that, Rue, and you didn't hear it."

I reached across to lay a hand on his arm. "It's fine," I told him gently. "Gatsby, Beasley, and I know to keep our lips firmly zipped. And ever since that day I went in for my checkup, I've wondered about that Berry Blast that Constance handed to Delilah."

Gatsby lay his head on Andy's lap, and Andy rubbed his fur.

"Does that mean you can tell where the poison came from—what kind of food or drink?" I asked.

Andy paused. "Let's just say we have a reason to believe that *some of it*, especially at the end, was likely introduced into Delilah's system in the form of drink," he said. "But we believe as well that she was poisoned over a period of time, with the poison possibly mixed into a variety of food and drink."

I paused to take that in: Delilah slowly being poisoned as she went about her happy life, spreading cheer to all the patients in the office where she worked. "But, Andy, *why?*" I cried. "That's what I want to know!" I said as Beasley nuzzled close into my chest. Clerical mistakes, possible nights out with a doctor who was seeing someone else...none of those made any sense as motives to end somebody's life. "Any clue about *why* someone would do a thing like that?" I asked.

Andy shook his head. "There are several theories. We are looking, for example, into the idea that it was someone from a neighboring community, who perhaps held an old grudge. As popular and energetic as she was, we are finding that Delilah had a circle of acquaintances that extended beyond our city limits. And she would frequently go into Eastham or Wellfleet for dinners and events and to visit friends."

I was dying to ask more about this possible old grudge. But Andy was divulging more than he ever did, and I wouldn't push my luck.

Then he seemed to ponder something before he finally spoke again. "Rue, let me ask you this, because you seem to have a knack for…happening upon crucial information in this case. Have you ever heard of a Theodore Oldingham?"

"Never heard of him. But I will, of course, let you know if I hear anything at all."

"And please keep that to yourself," he said with a nod.

I pulled an imaginary zipper tightly across my lips.

Theodore Oldingham. I repeated the name in my mind so I would not forget. Tonight I'd have a little talk with Google before I went to bed. As I finished up my wine, I made a silent promise to Delilah that the cops would catch the creep who took her life. And if I had to jump in with a little help, I was glad to be of service.

CHAPTER EIGHT

The next morning, we opened late since all the staff was eager to attend Delilah's funeral. Then I disappeared into my office, promising myself I would not come out until I chose four books to share on the podcast the next week along with three insightful quips.

But once the funeral crowd had finished with their lunches here in town, things got busy at the store, and I stepped out to help.

I approached a trio of teenage boys who had come in eagerly with their bingo cards in hand. "Welcome to the Seabreeze Bookshop," I told them with a smile.

One squinted at his card and then looked up at me. "Do you have…um…a yellow cat?" he asked.

"Or an emerald in the middle of a heart?" one of his friends jumped in to ask.

"I'm sorry," I replied. "But I hear a certain yellow cat gets a lot of cuddles from the surfers here in town, and I've had my eye on a gorgeous emerald necklace that is right next-door." We'd all been instructed to offer easy hints. After all, the whole point of the game was to send potential shoppers to Annie's Gallery, Surf's Up, and other stores in town.

"Excellent," said the first boy, a grin spreading across his face.

The third friend spoke up next. "And would you tell me, please, where I could find the Harry Potter books?"

"They're in our fantasy and science-fiction section, to your right and toward the back," I said. And since I understood that reading was not on this boy's mind, I nodded toward the tea stand. "But I believe that our friend Harry misplaced something over there when he last got some tea. It's something that he'll need if he wants to do some magic."

The boy could see the wand from where he stood, and it was apparently all he needed to form a complete line on his card. "Bingo!" he exclaimed. "Thank you so, so much."

The others looked at him with a mix of congratulations and a touch of jealousy.

"Congratulations, man," one told him with a sigh.

I stamped the little square, which would allow the player to collect the ten dollars he had earned in "Downtown Bucks." The prize would go to the first fifteen players to take their completed cards to Constance at the florist shop. I wished all of them good luck as they rushed out the door.

When business hit a lull, I pulled out my phone. I had been too tired the night before to search for information on Theodore Oldingham. Plus, I had frankly become exasperated with the maze of clues that simply made no sense—and that seemed to point to one suspect then another.

But no matter how impossible the clues, the case was about Delilah, and she deserved an answer.

The first thing Google pulled up was an obituary. Theodore, it seemed, had died the year before at the age of fifty-three. A father of three and an accountant, he had lived in nearby Yarmouth, and no cause of death was listed.

With that information, I added "Yarmouth" to the search bar but didn't find a single thing that could connect him to Delilah. He had led a hiking club, and he had been honored shortly before his death for organizing volunteers to clean up the trails. A photo showed a tall man with short gray hair and glasses smiling at the camera as he accepted the award.

There were ways, of course, to find out more. I could sign up for a hike with the Sunshine Striders Club and get to know the others Theodore had hiked with. Since Lester was unhappy with my lack of exercise, how thrilled would he be if I joined a hiking club!

The person who would not be thrilled was Andy. I thought about it for a moment. I had promised him I wouldn't say a word about what we had talked about. I hadn't promised not to hike!

Still, to contact the club would go against the spirit of the understanding that we had, and the last thing I'd ever want to do was to hurt the investigation.

But what was the connection between this man and Delilah? I was lost in thought when Stacey came in for her shift, taking her place behind the desk to pack up more orders.

"Hi, Stacey. How's it going?" I set down my phone and grabbed some books for her. This week had been our biggest yet for orders out of state.

Elizabeth walked over to straighten a display of chocolates that were shaped like classic books with the titles written out in icing.

"I think we may have to lower the price on those

things," I told her with a sigh. "They aren't all that popular."

"But they're adorable!" said Stacey.

"Oh, they are," I said. "From what customers tell me, they get an A-plus in design and a C at best for taste. And one doesn't put down money for a piece of chocolate because it's nice to look at." I was always grateful when customers were honest with me; it kept me from spending money on merchandise that would ultimately disappoint.

The cats, snoozing behind the desk, woke up from their naps and wound their way around my legs, rubbing their heads against my shins.

"Delilah told me once that she thought these tasted great." Elizabeth studied a chocolate made to look like an edition of *Pride and Prejudice*.

"What did Delilah *not* love?" I asked with a laugh.

"A lot of things, I guess," said Elizabeth. "But she was too nice to admit it. Do you remember when Ruth Carson made that Chocolate Oreo Delight for the Christmas bake-off?"

Stacey winced. "Is that the one she made with two cups of salt instead of sugar? I took one bite—and wow."

"Yes!" said Elizabeth. "And when Delilah noticed Ruth was about to cry, Delilah ate this whole big piece that she had on her plate."

"I cannot imagine," I said as I wrapped up an order.

"And," Elizabeth continued, "Delilah somehow did it with a smile on her face. 'Yum, yum,' Delilah said. I never will forget it as long as I live."

I laughed at the memory as Stacey grabbed another book to wrap.

"The only thing that I ever knew to displease Delilah was a strawberry-shortcake cupcake that someone, I suppose, had brought into the doctor's office," Stacey said. "It was just the cutest thing—with a fondant flower on the top. I had come in to clean, and Delilah took a bite as she was closing up. And, oh, the face she made." She smiled to herself as she wound some mailing paper around a hardback book. "Right away, of course, she stopped puckering up her lips and said the cupcake was 'divine.' But it must have tasted nasty if it broke through that armor of politeness Delilah always had."

With the poisoning on my mind, I was on alert. "When was this?" I asked.

"About six weeks ago or so."

The others didn't know that the cause of death had been confirmed as poisoning—and that the fateful bites and sips had been taken bit by bit over a period of time. Not to give up Andy's secrets, I tried to tamp down my eagerness for answers about this strawberry shortcake cupcake.

"Do you know who made it so we can avoid her cooking?" I busied myself by straightening up the counter. "Do we know the identity of the worst cook in Somerset Harbor?"

"She didn't say," said Stacey. "It was wrapped up by itself with a little ribbon. And because of that, I got the idea someone had brought in just the one cupcake for Delilah. It's not like there was a whole tray of the things back there in the kitchen." She let out a bray of a laugh. "Thank goodness for that, right?" She picked up some mailing labels. "People did that sometimes, you know—brought in treats for just Delilah. Because you couldn't help but love her," she said with a sigh.

Oh, yes, people loved her—except when their patience was running short and they were exasperated with her; it had gone to both extremes.

The bell on the door signaled a customer, and Elizabeth looked up. "Good times ahead," she said under her breath.

"Perfect," whispered Stacey as we noticed Constance coming through the door. Stacey dealt with Constance more than most, cleaning at the florist weekly and helping with deliveries when things got extra busy at An Elegant Bouquet.

With our hands hidden by the counter, Elizabeth and

I played a quick game of Rock, Paper, Scissors to see who had to wait on the new arrival.

Unfortunately, scissors cut into paper, and I made my way to the front. "So good to see you, Constance," I said.

The cats, fine judges of character that they are, became blurs of white and gray as they disappeared into my office.

I took a breath for courage and gave Constance my best smile.

The scowl on her face was my first indication she had not come in for books.

CHAPTER NINE

*a*s often was her way, Constance skipped the hello and got straight to business. "Am I to understand that you were closed this morning for two hours?"

What nerve the woman had. Her position as head of the merchants guild did not give her the right to dictate the hours that I kept.

But I kept my cool. "Yes, all of us at the Seabreeze Bookshop wanted to attend the service and pay our respects to Delilah."

"And if a customer came by?"

"Well, there is rarely an emergency that brings a customer into a bookstore, Constance. And most of the town, in fact, was at the church while we were briefly closed." I crossed my arms over my chest. "As much as I strive to make a profit, what was important to us this morning was the loss of someone we loved."

"Hmph." Constance got that look, like she smelled something rank.

"Now that I think about it, I didn't see you there."

Her nose shot up in the air as if it were being pulled by some unseen force. "I have a duty, Rue, to the customers I serve to be behind the desk at my posted business hours. Besides, it's not like we lost a saint. A lot of people suffered because of Delilah's carelessness. Lester never should have given her a job involving people's health. Because without our health, well, then we have nothing."

I noticed that Gatsby had appeared quietly to stand guard.

"Now that you have weighed in about my schedule, can I help you with something else? Because if not, I shouldn't chat. Duty to my customers, operating hours, all of that."

"I'm afraid there is another matter I must speak with you about," she said. "It has come to my attention that the bingo game has gone awry. And now it falls to me to visit every merchant listed on the cards to see where the issues lie. People seem to be getting too creative with the bingo clues—when the rules are very clear."

Having just buried one of our own, I highly doubted any merchants had spent a lot of time messing with some game. But no use to explain a thing like that to someone with no heart.

"Harry Potter's sword is still in place in the spot approved by you," I said, nodding in that direction. "You are welcome to walk over and inspect the thing up close, but I have work to do."

She sighed. "I know to some I must seem rigid. But this is for the good of all the merchants—to bring in extra business. As well as to provide a little fun for shoppers. But some of the participants are behaving as if it is a joke. Barney at the shoe store was supposed to put a plate of cookies at his register. A little snack for players! And a chance for some of them to mark off 'Something Sweet' if that square was on their cards." Fire formed behind her eyes. "That should be simple, right? But what did Barney do? Instead of a plate of cookies, he puts out a photograph of Kara at the stationery store! With 'sweet' spelled out in candy hearts—like bingo is some fancy way to announce his crush. This is a professional promotion that I'm running and not a dating service."

I thought it was kind of clever, and what could it hurt? The players who dropped by the store could still have their square stamped.

Constance wasn't finished yet. "And after all the signage for the clues has been approved, some know-it-all goes and writes one of the signs in French! Just to show off, I suppose!"

That one got my attention. Could it be the same "know-it-all" who had been prowling in Delilah's garden when they dropped that note?

I was about to ask Constance who it was when her cell phone buzzed and she marched out of the store, speaking sternly to someone who she called a "fool."

Never in my life would I expect to be sorry to see Constance take her leave. But I had to know who had written out their bingo clue in French.

Thankfully the store was quiet, so I told Elizabeth I had to run out on an errand. Then I rushed out the door before I lost sight of Constance.

First, she stopped at the surf shop, where she approved the clue for the square that read, "Yellow Cat." Felix was deep into his nap in his normal spot of sun next to the front door. But just in case he was not around in person when a player stopped in, a photo of the cat was displayed on the counter.

Needing to stay out of sight, I turned my back to the counter, pretending to examine the sunglasses display. I rushed toward the door when I sensed that Constance was about to leave, but it was too late.

"Taking more time off from the store, I see." She raised a brow at me. "I didn't know you surfed."

"I was told it was important I get some exercise," I said.

And then she was off, with me following at what I hoped was a safe distance.

Next on her list, apparently, was Sophisticated Soaps —where I didn't dare go in after my encounter at Surf's Up. Luckily, Patsy had left the door standing open to catch the sea-kissed breeze, and there was a bench outside where I could sit and listen.

It wasn't long before I heard Constance raise her voice. "This is supposed to say 'Touch of Lavender,' not 'Touche de Lavande.' How can players play the game if they can't read the clue?"

"Perhaps the sprig of lavender beside the box of soap is a sufficient clue?" asked Patsy, keeping her voice calm and even. "No one has missed it yet. I've initialed lots of little boxes on lots of bingo cards. You have to learn to give people credit."

"And *you* have to learn how to follow rules," said Constance. "My headaches with you people will simply never end. I have to stop in at the hobby shop, where I hear there's trouble. And then I will be off to the Museum of Science, where the ladies have been dropping off their baked goods for the end-of-bingo celebration. That museum director said she'd put up an ad about the need for food, but did she do it? No! So now I have to make sure enough people got the word to bring in sweets. Or else our guests will arrive to find an empty table, and what kind of celebration would that be?"

"Oh, I'm sure it's fine," Patsy reassured her. "In fact, I've heard the basement of that place is just *full* of cupcakes. We all know how it is. The ladies in this town jump at any chance to show off their specialties."

Full of cupcakes. Hmm. Might one of those specialties be strawberry-shortcake cupcakes topped with fondant flowers?

Before Constance could charge out of the store, I hurried to the Museum of Science, hoping I could peruse the sweets before the bingo czar finished terrorizing Stan at the hobby shop.

Ten minutes later, I was strolling through the heavily air-conditioned modern building with its displays about marine life and the natural surroundings of our part of Massachusetts. I went straight to the basement, home of the infrequently visited exhibit that was titled "Which Shell Could This Be?" Toward the back, a door was cracked open to a darkened room, and I slipped in, thankful to have the whole basement to myself. Inside the small room, a huge display of sweets was spread out across a table with items wrapped in plastic, sealed in baggies, and nestled into disposable foil dishes. The ladies of Somerset Harbor had indeed come through.

Knowing time was of the essence, I turned on the light and quickly scanned the table for any cupcakes that might have a pinkish tint. And there they were in the middle, a large plate of tiny cakes that exactly matched the one with the off-putting taste Stacey had described. And if that was not enough, taped across the top was a note: "Strawberry Shortcake Cupcakes—Patsy Kettles."

My hand flew to my chest as Patsy seesawed to the top of my suspect list. She loved to talk in French and she had likely made a cupcake that had caused the poisoning victim to recoil not long before her death.

But there was no time to ponder. There were footsteps close by, and then came the sound of Constance berating someone on the phone.

Quasimodo's Bells.

I quickly turned the light off and hurried out into the main room of the basement. With Constance between me and the exit, I had no choice but to pretend to be immersed in the shell exhibit.

Constance stared me down. "Quite the woman of leisure today, aren't we?"

"Just a bit of research." I slid open the little window

that revealed the name of two dainty oblong shells. "These are called Angel's Wings. Who knew? Now both of us are a little smarter than we were before." I met her sneer with a stern look of my own as I made my escape.

CHAPTER TEN

*T*hat night, with so many questions swirling in my mind, I loaded Gatsby into the car and headed to the beach. Puzzling out the murder seemed impossible, but I could take care of my body, strengthen my bones and muscles, and increase my energy as directed by the doctor.

"A lot of people," he'd told me, "pay big bucks to join a gym, but you and I, we have the beach! Get out there and enjoy!" I had wondered that day if the pep talk had been for himself as well. Judging from his pale complexion, he hadn't seen a lot of sun. And his walk had been slow and shuffling as he moved to his computer to consult my chart.

I could always count on Lester to tell it like it was. Anytime I tried to put off a screening or a shot, he'd give me that look. "If you were my daughter, Rue, I'd insist you make that a priority on your calendar this month." He made every one of us feel like we were family, and because of that, we chose carrots over french fries every now and then. And on nights when a cool breeze broke the heat and sent leaves flying at our feet, we called for our dogs, and we took that walk.

Once my furry friend and I got to the shoreline, I couldn't help but smile as Gatsby flew ahead of me then circled back to keep me company at my much slower pace.

This was Gatsby's happy place, and for me it was the place I could let my thoughts run free. Hopefully the fresh air and the pounding of the ocean waves could soothe the uneasiness that was now a hard ball in my stomach. Maybe here my mind could settle, and I could make some sense of the random threads of a confusing week.

I tried to simply breathe as I walked close enough to the rushing tide that it almost touched my sneakers. But as the first threads of pink began to ease across the sky, my mind wandered to the case. And I marveled at the secrets the murder had revealed along the pristine sidewalks and behind the quaint storefronts of our close-knit town.

Where the owner of my favorite coffee shop apparently was stalking the backyard of her late romantic rival. While the finely dressed purveyor of elegant high-end soaps had baked a suspicious-tasting cupcake for a murder victim.

And all of that was possibly to maintain the attention of an ordinary-looking doctor whose white coat was always stained with coffee and whose ears stuck out from his head like the handles of a jug.

In the meantime, down the sidewalk at the floral shop, the head of the merchant's guild might be guilty of something so much worse than domineering the store owners with her glares and her demands.

Just the thought of Constance made me walk a little faster. Lester would be pleased—I was almost at a jog!

How dare that woman think she had a right to an opinion about when I closed the store to allow my staff to attend a funeral. As I leaned toward one suspect and then another, it was Constance's attitude that sometimes nudged the florist to the top of the list. With a variety of suspects, only Constance seemed to have the cold and callous disregard for others that a killer would possess. There were times I sensed in her an anger that ran deeper than missed committee meetings and someone's failure to comply with the list of approved browns and beiges for improvement projects.

I pictured the glare she'd aimed at Delilah that day in

the office. "If looks could kill..." I'd thought. Not knowing then, of course, my friend was slowly being poisoned.

But there were also times I could almost swear there was a heart hiding behind the scowl Constance always wore. Sometimes I sensed she truly meant to help—in her own misguided way—by overwhelming the poor merchants with her "directives for enhancement of the downtown area."

On those days I was convinced that the purple shake had been simply meant to "wake up" Delilah's memory and not to finish up the job of slowly killing her. Constance was, after all, a florist. She was in the business of nourishing and growing, not the cutting away of life.

Constance was a whiz with flowers, and I pondered that a moment as oranges and reds mixed with the pink in the sky. Could someone be truly evil when they understood the way to create a little magic by placing tiny white carnations so exquisitely against the rich blue of delphiniums? To admit that was true, I'd have to believe as well that the authors of the best books on my shelves might, in fact, be people I wouldn't want to know. And it would kind of kill me to think that of my idols, the ones who wrote the lines that made me pause to take a breath and then read the words again.

Plus, what would be her motive? Andy had told me once his basic strategy was to analyze the motive and opportunity of each suspect on his list and then go with his gut to narrow down the list.

As I watched Gatsby bat at a piece of driftwood, I tried to think of anything that might link Constance to the murder of Delilah. There was the bingo game, of course, and the women's planning lunches—with the opportunity, perhaps, to slip a little something into Delilah's soup or salad dressing if she slipped off to the restroom.

Oh, and I'd forgotten that the two of them very briefly had their own little club to discuss non-fiction books. Who would have ever thought of the two of them as a pair, the bubbly Delilah and the no-nonsense Constance? It had all begun when they—and only a few others—showed up at my store for an author talk the year before.

Low turnouts were my constant fear when an author, at my invitation, took the time to prepare a talk and travel to the store. But on that night Peter Donnell had made the best of it and led a spirited discussion of his book, *How What You Learned in Science Class Can Make Your Garden Grow.*

I had used his presentation as a way to explore the possibility of forming a new special-interest book club at the store. We had groups for literary fiction, thrillers, and romance. And with all the gardeners and outdoors enthusiasts in town, I thought it might be nice to add a non-fiction club with a nature focus.

Well, that caught the interest of two people only in the audience that day. One of them was Constance, who apparently held a master's degree in geology from UMass in Amherst. The other was Delilah, who never met a topic that didn't catch her interest. It was at her suggestion that we began with a book on how to identify native birds.

Since the book club, in the end, didn't make the cut at the store, Constance and Delilah met on their own for a while, discussing books at a small restaurant that adjoined the Wainwright family farm. Constance used to tell me she appreciated the sensible prices Marcia Wainwright always charged without skimping on the portions.

"Marcia understands it shouldn't take a second mortgage to buy a decent piece of fish with a nice dessert," she told me more than once. (Even a compliment from Constance came in the form of an insult to someone somewhere.)

Those lunches, as I understood it, lasted several months—which meant an exploratory trip to the Wainwrights' restaurant might just be in order. Maybe

Marcia could remember something that had caused a conflict between Constance and Delilah. *Motive, opportunity,* said Andy in my head.

Plus, there was something else...something else about Delilah that I had forgotten. I knew it was there, dancing at the very edges of my thoughts, but what exactly was it? I seemed to think it somehow had to do with Constance. But for now the memory was lost, except for a vague sense of wrongness I'd felt at the time. Then, as always happens, life had handed me a series of other matters to capture my attention, and that small bit of drama was soon replaced with other things to occupy my thoughts.

As I tried to remember, Gatsby found a friend, a friendly-looking terrier who seemed to be his perfect match; both of them were obsessed with tearing around the beach in delirious and endless circles. I sat down in the sand and watched them play while the guys who'd brought the terrier threw a football back and forth.

When the dogs grew tired of playing, Gatsby's little buddy ran to me and sprawled out on his back to ask for tummy rubs. I happily obliged and then stood up; it was time to head back home.

"What's for supper, boy?" I asked an exhausted Gatsby as we strolled toward the car. I had the makings for a salad and some pesto sauce for chicken, but aromas from a nearby seafood restaurant filled the air, suggesting other ways to satisfy the appetite that I'd worked up.

Was that lobster I was smelling?

And that is when it hit me; that is when I finally grabbed hold of that elusive memory. There had been a note in the drop box at the store regarding the selection of the queen for the local Lobster Fest.

The note had been about Delilah.

And what a note it had been.

CHAPTER ELEVEN

*W*hile it had been unsettling at the time, the note had mainly left me puzzled. Now, given the tragedy that had followed, it took on an urgency. Thank goodness I'd remembered. I had to find that note.

At first it had only seemed like a slightly more dramatic version of the usual drama that surrounded the election of the Queen of the Lobster Fest. The title went to someone who was beloved for their contributions to the community, and they received a lobster dinner as well as a nice plaque. Constance had assigned me to take charge of setting up the voting process, and votes came in online as well as being placed in a drop box at my store.

The anonymous note I found inside the box one

evening had left me more confused than alarmed. But something had told me I should save it, and I really hoped I could find it now. The most important things—like my warranties and passport—seemed to sometimes end up in the oddest places, where I thought they would be "safe."

After the short walk home, I filled Gatsby's bowls and rushed up to my room, all thoughts of food forgotten. I flipped through the pages of my rare edition of *Pride and Prejudice.* I checked inside the vintage luggage I'd stacked in front of my bed as a fun touch. Both hiding places held some papers that were important to me—but no note.

Then, luckily, there it was, tucked in with some letters in the bottom drawer of a jewelry box. I unfolded it and read.

If people only knew the truth about what Delilah did, they'd know that Delilah is not any kind of queen. The truth is so much uglier than most people know—uglier than causing careless mix-ups with appointments. And does Delilah flatter herself to believe it is truly "love" between her and "her" man? Just ridiculous!

My heart began to race, because I knew this "truth" might just be the thing that had been behind Delilah's death. But there was no hint about what that truth could have been. I studied the note, whose neat and careful letters seemed at odds with the furor that the writer had been obviously feeling.

It struck me that the writer also seemed to know about the women Lester was rumored to be dating, which wasn't common knowledge. Or at least I hadn't known! And a *lot* of things got shared at the tea cart at the Seabreeze.

The title of queen that year had gone to Ellen Cason, who ran the front office of Somerset Harbor Elementary like the boss she was while making sure the school was a safe and happy place for kids. No one could argue Ellen did not deserve the honor, but I'd heard a lot of buzz about Delilah, and I had been surprised to find the votes had not come out in her favor.

In the box at my store, at least, Delilah had seemed to be way ahead. I had wondered then if Constance might have messed with the count, as much control as she liked to wield over every single thing. But then I decided that, as much as some of the ladies loved the drama of the contest, an election for Lobster Queen would have almost been beneath Constance's notice. She'd have been more concerned about the profits that came in from the event.

But every single year, people took surprisingly hard

lines on who should and who should not reign as Lobster Queen. They behaved as if the holder of that title decided consequential things for the future of the town. Instead, she simply got to wear a bright red crown while taking the first ceremonial bite of lobster to mark the start of the event.

At the time, I'd thought the note was simply a result of some silly jealousy. But given the dark course of events that had followed, the P.S. gave me chills.

Delilah Bradenton knows exactly what she did, and it is abominable.

CHAPTER TWELVE

he next day I tried to force myself to get my mind on work. I wrote down some ideas for the podcast, suggesting that the listeners pair a shiny new read with a companion book. With so many historical fiction titles coming out, they might find it fascinating to pair their favorite with a work of well-reviewed non-fiction. I began some research to find pairings that focused on the same period of time or the same real-life events.

The sales floor soon got busy, and customer requests sometimes pulled my thoughts from the work at hand—and also from the tone of the bitter note, which still haunted me.

Abominable? How could anybody use that word in connection with *Delilah,* who was big-hearted to a fault?

And then it hit me with a force. I'd heard Constance use that word a lot. Usually in connection to what she considered the most grievous offense of us merchants: the failure, for example, to sweep in front of our stores "in a timely fashion."

I was very curious to know what Andy thought. I'd called him earlier, but he had been too busy to hear about what I had remembered. I'd heard a lot of buzz behind him at the station and had strained to see if I might pick up some information. I'd made out Delilah's name as well as some talk about "financial issues"—which went with exactly *none* of the theories that I had. She'd always seemed to have enough to live quite comfortably, and while she'd loved pretty clothes, she had been a fan of bargains and "fun" prints rather than designer labels.

When the surge of customers finally hit a lull, I checked my phone again to see if Andy had called back as he'd promised, but there were no messages or texts.

It was like a real-life game of Clue. Patsy with the pink cupcake? Judy with a latte? Or might it have been Constance with the purple drink?

And what was all this talk about financial troubles? The questions nagged at me as I picked up some of the books the customers had not reshelved. I could only dive in to explore one question or suspect at a time.

And I knew just the place to explore more deeply the relationship between Constance and Delilah. Had the two of them had conflicts that were deeper than we knew?

"Elizabeth," I said as she passed me with a stack of books, "how would you like to grab some lunch with me a little later at Wainwright's?" It could be a double win: the possibility of answers plus Marcia Wainwright's famous white beans with kale and wild rice.

Elizabeth looked thoughtful. "You know, I haven't thought of that place in a while," she said. "It's a bit of a drive, but it would be a nice change. And their food is always fresh." Most of the ingredients came directly from Marcia and Daryl Wainwright's farm across the street from the white clapboard restaurant. When the four Wainwright children were old enough to go to school, Marcia had opened Wainwright's as a way to supplement the family's income and prepare for those four college tuitions she knew were in her future.

Two hours later, Elizabeth pulled her Jeep into the lot of the small white converted home that housed the eatery —or that used to, anyway. Wainwright's, apparently, had recently become a combination of a store and...some kind of spiritual retreat?

The collection of hand-painted signs along the sidewalk just confused me more.

Jams and Jellies!

Free Your Mind!

You Are Enough!

Baby Goats!

"*You are enough?* And *Goats?*" Elizabeth frowned as she slowed to a stop. "No *Fresh Corn!* Or *Pasta Primavera?*" She let out a groan. "That corn was the best."

"Well, let's say hello, at least." I opened the passenger-side door, and we climbed up the red painted steps that led to the familiar wooden sign with *Wainwright's* spelled in black.

On the drive to lunch, I had meant to explain my real reason for the visit. But she had needed to discuss a problem with an order, and time just got away.

We entered a neat and spacious room, taking in the neat shelves of merchandise. Among other things, I spotted fresh cheeses, brightly colored peppers, and soft-looking throws in a variety of hues. Some birdhouses and pottery filled a shelf in the back marked "Local Artists."

This for sure was not a restaurant, but it did look like a place I would like to shop when my mind was not so scattered. Business, it seemed, was good, and almost every aisle had browsers.

Marcia was in the middle of a knot of female customers, and soon she broke away, flashing us a big smile as she brushed a black curl from her eyes. "So good to see you both!" she said. "Elizabeth and Rue! It has been a while."

I nodded. "Long enough that we had no idea you'd made a change."

Elizabeth gave her a sheepish grin. "I was kind of hoping you'd have apple pie and maybe lentil soup," she said.

"Oh, I do sell mini pies, and I believe we still have some apple, although those go fast." Marcia nodded toward a case of baked goods, that did look delightful. "I did love the restaurant," she told us quietly. "But the competition made it tough. In the tourist season, we'd have lines right out the door, but the other months were hard. So I came up with a new plan, and so far so good." Indeed, things seemed to be very busy as she waved to a customer who was heading out the door with a bag of apples.

"I am light," called out the woman in the casual kind of way someone else would say goodbye.

But that made no sense. I must have heard her wrong.

"I choose happiness," Marcia called out happily in response to the customer's odd remark. Then she touched my hand. "We are all light and love!" she explained. "And it is part of my job to help the people who come here find the light inside themselves. It is so much more fulfilling than simply serving lunch! Now I feed souls and spirits and not only people's stomachs."

Another customer turned toward us with some pink wool in her hand. "Is this your first time?" she asked us. "It's such a special place. I just feel so loved here by both Marcia and Alonzo." With that, she blushed a little, her face turning the light pink shade of her wool.

I was so confused. "So! You found romance?" I asked. "Along with your…supplies for crafting?"

The woman giggled. "Well, I would not say that," she said, exchanging an amused look with Marcia. "Alonzo is a goat! But just the sweetest little goat you ever met!"

What in the world had this place become and how did goats fit in? I was so confused. Oh well; it sounded nice.

"The two of you should join us sometime for a class," said Marcia. "In addition to a store, this is a yoga studio."

"Yoga with baby goats!" the customer explained.

Hmm. I had heard that in some places goat yoga was a thing. And I imagined that the tourists (as well as stressed-out locals) might be eager to sign up, filling this place up even more.

Marcia had always seemed the quiet, unassuming

type, but I was reassessing. Maybe Marcia was a genius when it came to business. Even now she seemed to be in a hurry as a customer waved her over with a question.

All of this was good, but there still was the matter of getting any information she might have about Delilah's conversations with Constance at the restaurant. And now was not the time with so many customers needing her attention.

"Goat Yoga! We'll be there!" I decided as Elizabeth stared at me, surprised. I wished I'd had a chance to tell her in the car why I really needed to grab some time with Marcia.

"Can I get a schedule from you?" I asked Marcia, who looked pleased.

"We've just added some new classes," she informed me as she pulled a schedule from the desk. "More people lately seem to have found the need for some inner calm, which we all could use. Especially after that business with Delilah, which just breaks my heart."

She held up a finger to the customer to signal she'd be over in one minute. Then she lowered her voice. "You know, I saw Delilah about six weeks ago when we drove into Boston for a play. It was a fine production of *A View from the Bridge*—you know, by Arthur Miller—and she was there with Lester Holmes. I just could not get over how happy Delilah seemed that night! And Patsy was there too." Marcia shook her head. "What a coincidence. It was like all of Somerset Harbor had made the trip to Boston that one night for the play."

Bridge. I had a strong sense that I'd heard that word in another context that could be important.

I tried to think about it in the car on the way back to the bookstore. But Elizabeth was chattering away about some confusing thing that had happened in her childhood that left her afraid of goats.

"Afraid of goats?" I asked. Good grief. As she pulled up to a stoplight, I reached into my Wainwright's bag and handed her a mini pie.

"Plus, yoga is for people who are more flexible than me!" Elizabeth protested. "I've been known to lose my balance when I tie my shoe. That's how inflexible I am."

"I can't imagine anything less scary than a baby goat," I said, holding back a laugh.

"Well, it was Halloween," she said, "and some of the other kids thought it would be funny to dress the goat up like a pirate. Which sounds adorable, I know, but I was only four. I had nightmares for a month." She took a bite of pie before the light turned green.

"It will be fine," I said, but my mind was not on goats. I had just remembered why the title of the play had triggered something in my mind. "That play Marcia mentioned!" I said to Elizabeth. "It had *Bridge* in the title, and remember what you told me about Patsy? And how she was so furious that day about Delilah?"

"Yes!" The connection was now clear to Elizabeth as well. "I thought it was all about something she had seen —or heard—on some bridge somewhere. But it must have been about her running into Lester and Delilah together at that play."

A View from the Bridge.

Elizabeth continued, "I honestly wasn't paying much attention at the time to the part about the bridge." She brushed a crumb from her blouse. "I was just so startled about how angry Patsy was—and the way she just assaulted Delilah's character."

And that had been a few months ago, right about the time the poisoning could have started. Andy had let it slip that the cops were thinking it had happened over a period of weeks or months.

The car ride was quiet after that with both of us deep in thought.

CHAPTER THIRTEEN

wo days later the sun was shining on us as I drove Elizabeth back to Wainwright's on a late Wednesday afternoon. That was typically a slower time of the week at the store, so we had left things in the hands of my two part-timers.

Elizabeth was going under protest. "Do you know that some people, Rue, are actually allergic when it comes to goats?" she asked. "And I did sneeze a lot in those early years before my family moved off the farm and into town."

"You'll do just fine," I said, "and it could be fun. Not to mention we will hopefully have the chance to talk to Marcia for a bit." I had filled in Elizabeth about why I wanted to pick Marcia's brain about Constance and Delilah.

A group of about twelve women had gathered by the time we walked onto the grassy area next to the store where we'd been told to meet. After we grabbed some mats, I glanced around at the others, who, like us, were dressed in leggings and comfy-looking tops. A couple of ladies were doing stretches, extending one arm into the air and then another. One woman to my left moved her head from side to side to stretch her neck. Figuring it couldn't hurt, I did the same.

Soon, Marcia strode out smiling from around the corner, her curls pulled back into a tight ponytail. "Welcome ladies!" she said. Then she clasped her hands together, her smile growing even bigger. "Once again, I think we have some friends who'd like to come out and say hello," she said. She opened a gate to send a large group of baby goats bouncing out into the yard.

As the women squealed and clapped, a white goat ran up to me, nuzzling my knee. I smiled, feeling chosen, as I reached down to pet him. Then, before I knew it, a black goat with white ears was romping around me in a circle as Marcia got us started.

First, she reminded us to breathe in deeply, keeping our breath slow and steady. "The way we breathe can affect our nervous systems and our heart rates," she told the class, and I marveled at how Marcia's yoga voice could instantly ease the storm that had been brewing in me.

Then she instructed us to find an "inner center" of calm within ourselves. "Focus on this moment," she told us quietly. "Do not be distracted by what you left undone or what you still have to do. Focus on the smell of the grass, the little bit of breeze, the movement of your body as you bend and stretch. The now is what's important. Focus on the now."

After some basic stretches, the first pose was a half-bend forward.

So far so good, I thought.

Then we did a pose on the ground, extending our left legs behind us. It was at that point that I noticed a goat climb onto the back of my neighbor, where he remained throughout the pose.

The other goats milled playfully around the group, and I concentrated on holding my pose steady until I found myself nose to nose with a new goat friend. His gaze was a mix of "You can rock this yoga thing" and "Stop for a while and play."

As the goats climbed over and under us and snuggled up for cuddles, Marcia told us it was fine to stop and snap some pictures. "Animals do wonders to help us release stress, which is one of the major reasons people turn to yoga," she explained. "Stretch a little, play a little, laugh. All of it is good!"

During a trickier portion of the class, I found myself balancing unsteadily on one leg with my hands clasped above my head. I glanced at Elizabeth, who was holding her pose like a champ, despite the fact that a spotted goat had settled on her foot to take a nap. And I could tell by the little half-smile on her face that her fear of goats was gone.

Afterward, we waited for the crowd to dissolve, hoping to have a little quiet time with Marcia. I grabbed my water bottle and sat down next to Elizabeth, who was sprawled out in the grass with two goats in her lap. "You survived," I said.

"I did! But now I can't get up—because someone is asleep," she said. The spotted goat was nestled at her side, continuing his nap.

"If this was meant to calm us, Marcia might be onto something," I decided. "I am not nearly as hyped up as I was before."

We sat in the quiet, practicing our new skill: being in the moment. Then before long, Marcia joined us, and she took a seat on a nearby bench. "What did you ladies think?" she asked.

Elizabeth gave her a thumbs-up.

"I do hope you'll come back," said Marcia, sipping

from her water bottle. "This is such a nice group, and you two would fit right in."

I looked at Elizabeth, who nodded. "I think that would be nice," she said.

I was in as well; Lester would be pleased.

"You've built a fantastic business," I told Marcia as a goat rubbed his cold nose against mine. "But I have to say, I would love a great big helping of that creamed corn you used to make."

She smiled and let out a big sigh. "What I don't miss, Rue, is all that time in the kitchen. But the customers? Yes, I do miss the faces. We had a lot of regulars, and they were the best."

"Do you know what I remember?" I reached out to pet the goat, along with his goat friend who had just appeared at my side. "I had this bright idea once to start a discussion group—about books that dealt with science. Like, what was I even thinking?" I paused while the three of us enjoyed a laugh. "And when it turned out to be just Constance and Delilah, the bookstore group was canceled," I continued. "But the two of them kept going, and they'd come out to your restaurant to talk about the books. Do you remember that? How long did that go on?"

"They'd come every Tuesday right until we closed." A sad look crossed Marcia's face. "Oh, how we'll miss

Delilah! And when I think about the last few times the two of them were in, I want to strangle Constance. It seemed like toward the end, she was just so horrid when it came to Delilah." She paused for a moment. "Of course, I understand that Constance is just brusque as a matter of routine, but this was so much worse than her normal kind of awful."

Marcia shook her head. "The woman is a beast!" she said. "She'd criticize the proportion of starches versus healthy vegetables Delilah ordered for her lunch. More than once, I heard her tell Delilah she was nothing but a fool—when Delilah would fumble for her car keys or spill coffee on her dress." Marcia paused. "As opposed to the Constance I was used to seeing, her remarks on those days seemed to come from a place of anger rather than the sense of superiority that is usually her style."

"And you have no idea what had set her off?" asked Elizabeth.

"No, I really don't. At first the two got along okay, but then something seemed to happen, and I noticed a big change in the way that Constance treated her. And some days poor Delilah was on the verge of tears. She kept going on and on about some job or another she'd applied for—and how she was so sure she had blown the interview."

"Wait a minute. What?" I exchanged a glance with Elizabeth. "I don't understand. Delilah *had* a job."

"Oh." Marcia stared down at her gray sneakers. "If that wasn't common knowledge, I should have kept my mouth shut, I suppose. I thought everybody knew."

We were quiet for a moment, and I held my breath, hoping she'd tell us more.

Finally, she spoke. "I always kind of felt that was part of my job—to keep whatever secrets I might happen to pick up. You hear a lot of things when you stop by a table to refill the coffee or to offer extra rolls. And if it's private stuff, a conscientious server will keep it to herself."

I pushed some hair from my eyes, still dazed. "But Lester was so fond of Delilah! I just can't imagine that he would…" I let my voice trail off.

Whatever the nature of their relationship—romantic or platonic—Lester and Delilah had been close. He appreciated all the little extras Delilah did for patients. And in my time in the office, I'd observed the way they knew the smallest things about each other. Lester would let Delilah know when the soup of the day across the street was her favorite lemon orzo. And she would gently remind her boss when his hair needed a good trim.

"I honestly don't know what the story was on that,"

said Marcia as sadness filled her eyes. "I just know there was a lot of talk of jobs and where Delilah might go next."

In the silence that descended on our group, my thoughts turned to my last visit with Lester in his office. He had staunchly defended his receptionist when she'd been attacked that day by Constance. But he'd confided in me too that he was losing patients because of the constant mix-ups, messages not delivered, all the neglected tasks.

Lester had seemed stressed about the future of the practice. Had he been about to make a difficult decision when the unthinkable had happened?

"As much as we all adored Delilah, it makes sense in a way," mused Elizabeth. "There was a week last year when my migraines came back worse than they'd ever been. And Lester never got the three messages I left to call in my medication. I had to go for what seemed like forever before I got my pills. It was excruciating."

"On the other hand," I said thoughtfully, "I think some of the patients came to the office for Delilah almost more than Lester." She was always listening to somebody's marriage troubles. Or helping them decide how to entice their widowed mothers to get out of the house and interact with people. "I can see how he really needed things to run more smoothly in the office," I continued. "But he might have also lost a lot of patients if he let her go."

Marcia frowned and nodded. "There would have been an uproar."

"Rue, you have a point," said Elizabeth. "Either way he'd lose."

Unless something happened that meant he'd neither have to fire her or keep her behind the desk.

Which would have *only* been a motive for a lesser man than Lester. Still, my yoga-induced calmness had completely disappeared as I stood to go. "Well, this has been nice and all, but those books won't sell themselves," I said, prompting Elizabeth to gently disengage from her lap full of goats.

The two of us were quiet as we made our way to the car, trailed by a furry escort who seemed sad to see us go.

CHAPTER FOURTEEN

*a*ndy finally called back just as I finished with a customer who needed several books for a plane ride overseas.

Now that he was finally listening, I hesitated for a second. Where exactly to begin? I settled on the note I had remembered from the drop box. I explained the circumstances and told him what it said.

I could tell it piqued his interest, but he was rushed as usual. Someone from the station would be over to the house that night to get it, he informed me, if that would be okay.

"Sure. Anything to help," I said. "Oh! And I found out today that Patsy had seen Lester with Delilah at a play in Boston, which seemed to absolutely send her into orbit. Right about the time you think the poisoning began."

"Well, Rue, I hardly think—"

"Patsy after that went on a tirade about Delilah to Elizabeth. And then she nursed a grudge against Delilah up until she died, was just awful to her. At least, that's what Judy says."

"Well, yes, that's good to know." Andy sounded tired. "But if there is nothing else, Rue, I really have to go."

"Also, were you aware—and this blows my mind—that Lester had apparently let Delilah know that she should find another job?"

"*What?*"

I explained what I had learned after the yoga session.

"Now, that is interesting," said Andy, almost to himself. "And combined with the information from that latest witness and the statements from the creditors…" He did not complete the sentence, understanding quickly he had said too much. "I do appreciate the information, Rue," he said.

My mind began to spin with theories about the possible financial angle to the murder. But I knew not to ask.

"Andy, get some rest, and don't forget to eat," I said. I worried a lot about him when things revved up at work.

"I will do my best. And, Rue, while this has all been very helpful, I would appreciate it if you'd leave it to the cops to gather information from the witnesses and all. These things must be handled with the utmost care."

"All I was doing, Andy, was a little yoga, which promotes a healthy heart. It is also very calming. You should take a class." Then I had to suppress a giggle at the picture that created in my mind.

Andy cleared his throat. "Just be careful, Rue," he said, hanging up.

I stood behind the counter for a moment, mulling over Andy's slip. Had the "abominable" something in the note been related to finances? Since Delilah seemed in good shape with a nice home and modest spending, perhaps the "financial issues" I'd heard the cops discuss were related to the business. With patients bailing on the practice, had an unpaid debt put Delilah in harm's way? That theory seemed extreme—unless Lester had turned to some shady sources to try to get his numbers in the black.

I was pulled away from that thought by the sound of laughter coming from the corner where Elizabeth was working with her antique treasures.

"What's up?" I asked her, making my way over. I could use a laugh.

"Check this out," she said, handing me a photo, which I peered at with interest.

"Is that really Constance?" I asked Elizabeth. "Who knew that she could smile?"

The photo looked to be about two decades old. Constance and a tall man were loaded down with towels and a cooler with the beach in the background. They had turned around to laugh at something being said by whoever held the camera.

"You have to use this picture in your show," I told Elizabeth. "People won't believe what they are seeing here—Constance looking like a person you wouldn't run away from, Constance having fun."

Elizabeth added the photo to the lineup of "Best Friends Through the Years."

"But are we sure this was a best friend and not a romantic interest?" My eyes were still glued to the photo.

Elizabeth nodded toward the picture. "Read the back," she said.

I turned the photo over to read the description: "The dearest of friends. Yarmouth, 1998."

"That guy looks familiar," I said thoughtfully. "Something about the eyes."

"The eyes!" the parrot called. "1998!"

Then I had a hunch, perhaps a crucial one. I pulled my cell from my pocket and took a picture of the face of the mystery man.

Elizabeth scrunched her brow. "What are you doing, Rue?"

"A Google image search," I said, peering down at the results.

"Marley's Ghost!" I cried after a few minutes. "I *thought* it might be him. Constance was 'dear friends' with Theodore Oldingham."

"Theodore Olding*who?*" asked Elizabeth.

I nodded toward the photo. "This man is somehow mixed up with Delilah's case. Oh, and we have to keep that information just between me and you. Andy didn't tell me how this man might be relevant. But he was very interested in knowing if I'd ever heard his name."

"Oh, do you know what?" A spark lit up my best friend's face. "That last name rings a bell."

"Rings a bell!" echoed Zeke.

Elizabeth moved to her computer to look through some files and soon was nodding to herself. "A Lisa Oldingham got in touch with me a few months ago," she said, "to see if I had any photos or paraphernalia and the like from a certain club. A group that met here in the eighties to build and sail model boats."

"Hmm. I've never heard of that kind of club," I said.

"And I haven't either, so I couldn't really help," she said.

I pulled up the obituary I had found before, and there was Lisa's name. Theodore had been her father.

I smiled at Elizabeth. "You know, it would be so convenient if you could find some little gem that might be of interest to Lisa Oldingham." In deference to Andy, I wouldn't drive to Yarmouth to track down the friends and family of this Theodore. But I could not be blamed if one of his daughters walked into my store!

Elizabeth gave me a wink. "I'll see what I can do."

CHAPTER FIFTEEN

a little later in the day, I emerged from my office to catch sight of a familiar silver helmet of a hairdo. I wasn't in the mood to be "graced" with Constance Asher's presence, but it was what it was.

I watched her take a sip of Berry Blast as she gazed down at the table in Elizabeth's corner of the store.

Elizabeth smiled at me. "I just had to call Constance to come over and show her what I found," she said.

Constance looked down at the photo with a soft look in her eyes I'd never seen before. "This is exactly how I think of Theodore to this very day," she said. "He was like a brother to me, and I thank you, Elizabeth, for discovering this treasure."

I moved closer to them. "Tell me about him,

Constance." I studied the picture once again. "I can tell by looking at him he must be so much fun."

Of course, I might have said the same thing about the young Constance in the photo. Photos can hide truths, or people can become the very opposite of who they used to be. Or both things could be true.

"He was the best," said Constance.

"So, he is no longer with us?" I asked, playing dumb.

Constance took another sip of neon purple. "I lost him long ago." Her mouth tugged up just a little as she carefully picked up the photo. "But here he is again!" Then her demeanor changed back to the old Constance. All business once again, she turned to Elizabeth. "Please set this aside for me to purchase once your show is done."

"Let's just say it will be a gift—a gift from me to you!" said Elizabeth, and Constance looked as surprised by the gesture as I was.

"Well, that, I have to say, is no way to turn a profit," Constance barked, and then her voice grew quiet. "But that…is very kind."

"The collections that I curate are kind of about luck," Elizabeth told us thoughtfully. "Some box from an estate sale can be packed to the brim with a lot of useless stuff. Or stuck down in the bottom I might find…a little piece of magic, just the perfect thing a certain person needs to see." She shrugged. "And that just feels like something that's between the gods of fate and whoever's meant to have the photo or the letter or whatever." She shrugged. "For me to ask them for ten dollars almost seems a little gauche."

I gazed down at the picture. "I can tell how much the two of you just loved to be together, Constance. How did you two meet?"

"Theodore is not a subject that I talk about," she told us. "The end was just horrific, and no one was made to pay for the tremendous loss of an upstanding man." She scowled at the carpet as if it were the offender. "But our systems of justice," she continued, "are as much of a mess as the other so-called 'services' our government is supposed to provide."

Had to pay in what way? If this Theodore was murdered, that surely would have shown up in my Google search—unless the cops had considered it to have been an accident.

Was the murder of my own dear friend connected in some way to another murder? Or was the connection between Theodore and Delilah just some random dead end the cops had once pursued?

Hopefully, Elizabeth could find a reason to get the daughter on the phone since Constance wasn't talking.

Behind us, a mother pulled a book off the shelf for

her twins, who appeared to be four or so. "It's your favorite, Pat the Bunny," she told the little boys.

"That's my favorite too," I told them with a wink, then I turned to their mom. "Can I help you find something special?"

"Oh, thanks, but we'll just browse," she said, "and see what piques their interest."

And what seemed to interest them the most was not a book.

"Look at that lady's drink!" one twin shouted, pointing at the Berry Blast.

"She has a drink that glows!" The other stared, entranced.

"A magic drink!" his brother yelled.

"An *essential* drink," said Constance. "To improve your memory and focus and boost your energy."

Having decided the Berry Blast was boring after all, the boys went back to Pat the Bunny, and Constance turned to us. "I pick one of these up every day while I'm out and about. Both of you should try it; it tastes a little nasty, if I'm being honest, but it does the trick. It's a mystery to me why Judy doesn't sell more of these *useful* drinks instead of those frou-frou lattes."

"You get this Berry Blast from Judy?" asked Elizabeth. "I've never seen a smoothie on the menu at her place."

"It was something new she tried about a month ago at my insistence," Constance said. "Because there is just a dearth of healthy options at our establishments in town. Plus, a diversity of merchandise brings more money to the coffers!"

What a business sold—or didn't—was not for Constance to weigh in on. But this was interesting. The odd-looking drink that Delilah drank not long before her death had come from Judy's place!

"I've told Judy more than once she should promote the heck out of this thing, this miracle she sells." Constance raised her voice, holding up her drink. "But she insists her customers come in craving coffee and a hit of caffeine." She snorted in disgust. "What makes no sense to me is that lately, it's almost like she hides this thing on her menu. Like the Berry Blast is a dirty little secret."

Dirty little secret? Or perhaps a murder weapon?

As Gatsby's happy yelps signaled a customer, I took a cleansing breath and turned to welcome the newcomer.

CHAPTER SIXTEEN

After pointing the new customer to our Bargain Corner, I told Elizabeth I might make a coffee run to Whiskers and Coffee Beans. It was time, I thought, for another chat with Judy. And how convenient when one's sleuthing can be combined with caffeine in the form of creamy caramel delight.

Maybe it meant nothing. But I knew at least some of the poison at the end had come in the form of a drink. And the woman I'd caught stalking in Delilah's yard had mixed up a drink for the victim not long before she died.

"Perfect," said Elizabeth, holding her hand over her heart in delight. "Because a Cat's Meow Vanilla Cappuccino can improve my focus and energy just as much as some purple nonsense that tastes bad and hurts the eyes.

No matter what the head of the merchants guild believes."

"Oh, and by the way," I said, "that was pretty nice, what you did for Constance."

"Well, I got to thinking it's probably been a while since someone did something nice for her, you know? Which, I have to say, she brings on herself, but it seemed the thing to do." She straightened up a line of more best-friend pictures she'd pulled for her show. "I was kind of hoping she'd say more about her friend there in the picture," Elizabeth continued, "but hopefully there will be a good excuse to call the sister soon."

In fact, she'd found a sale going on that very week for the estate of a boat enthusiast and avid collector. It would be a long shot to find items about the specific club Lisa Oldingham had mentioned. But since the universe, according to Elizabeth, had handed down a gift for someone as mean as Constance, maybe it could help me too.

Fifteen minutes later, my head was exploding as I climbed the steps to Whiskers and Coffee Beans. I'd had to navigate past some high-decibel construction work, winding up and down side streets as crews did road repairs in front of Judy's place. Inside, I paused to rub the ears of a white kitten with black spots who was lying in a corner with his head on his paws. I sensed an air of sadness about the tiny creature, in contrast to the other cats, who were rushing past me, batting at a toy.

Something in the kitten's eyes caused me to kneel down and rub beneath his chin, which was Beasley's favorite place for me to pet. "It will be okay," I whispered, talking to myself as well as him. Andy or *someone* would solve this for Delilah, even if I had to help them do some digging.

Except for the noise outside, the coffee shop was quiet. There were only servers, who were gathered around as Judy placed miniature cups on a tray. Her hair was piled on top of her head, and she wore a light blue T-shirt that declared "All I Need Are Cats."

When she saw me, she smiled. "Rue! You've come on a good day. Would you like to help us sample some new items we might add to our menu? I want to step it up a bit around this place, and we've come up with some ideas."

"Sure. That could be fun." I was due for a treat.

She carefully moved the tray to a table near the counter. "It seemed like a good day for the staff to do a tasting," she explained. "I figured business would be slow since it is such an effort for people to find their way to us. With the road torn up and all." Then she clasped her hands together and looked around at her staff. "Is everybody ready?"

First up was a peppermint mocha coffee, which the staff deemed was too sweet, although I gave it a thumbs-up. (Too sweet? No such thing!) Next, Judy handed out a white chocolate raspberry option, which we all thought was perfect. That was followed by a series of coffee drinks from around the world, which Judy thought would add a fun touch to the menu. The one I liked the best was a wondrous concoction that involved vanilla ice cream mixed into the coffee, a supposed favorite of German coffee drinkers.

After we'd tasted for a while with Judy taking detailed notes, she and I moved to a corner table to catch up. I grabbed another German *eiskaffee* to bring along.

The tasting had been lucky in more ways than one; I had the perfect segue to ask about the purple drink that might have killed Delilah. "This was fun," I said as the spotted kitten wound around my feet. Settling by my chair, he assumed the same mournful position as before.

"Variety is good," I said, holding up my cup. "Oh, and by the way, someone was telling me they tried...some kind of purple health drink here? But maybe they were wrong. I don't see it on the menu, and it doesn't really fit with the coffee vibe." I picked up the kitten, who nuzzled against my chin. This baby was so tiny compared to the others.

"Oh! Well…yes, the purple drink." Judy watched the floor, seeming rather flustered.

In the silence that came after, I stroked the kitten's back, hoping Judy would continue. My eyes roamed the room, landing on a tall plant, where I noticed something odd. At first, I thought some yellow leaves had fallen into the potting soil—but then I looked more closely, and they were *grapefruit peels.*

I thought two things at once. First of all, how weird. And secondly, I noticed that these peels looked fairly fresh, unlike the shriveled ones I'd seen at Delilah's the day I saw Judy there. Those peels had been old—which meant our barista extraordinaire had been in Delilah's yard on another day as well, randomly tossing citrus peels wherever they might land. It had to have been her. How many citrus-peel tossers could there be? This was the kind of town where most people used our trash cans in the proper way.

And she had not been there to innocently stroll the yard with Delilah before Delilah died. If Delilah had been present, Judy would have never tossed the trash from her snack among Delilah's beloved plants.

What had she been searching for?

As I was mulling that over, Judy finally found her

voice. "Well, about the drink. Kind of off-brand for me, and I just did it, really, to get Constance off my back. So, if she comes in, I make it. And it's really no big deal."

Except her face told me there was more.

"Oh, okay, I get it." I met Judy's eye. "Constance is a pain. It just seems curious, I guess, that it's not up there on the menu. Which might be a good idea, don't you think, if it's something that you make?" I shrugged. "You might sell a lot. Who knows?"

Judy cleared her throat. "I'd just rather not, okay?"

What exactly was the deal? Had the cops identified the drink as a murder weapon? Something about the Berry Blast had for sure spooked Judy.

Her phone pinged at that point, and she looked down to read a text. "That's Patsy," she told me, "hoping we can go out tomorrow for a drink. Poor Patsy's had it rough."

"Yeah, it must be tough to be on the outs with a friend who suddenly is…gone," I said with a sigh.

"It's been hard," said Judy. "And that's not the only thing. There have been a lot of issues in the past year or so that have caused all kinds of turmoil for our Patsy." She frowned and shook her head. "Things that wouldn't mean a thing to the likes of you and me." She leaned back in her chair and raised a brow as she continued. "You would have thought the world had ended when they discontinued the hair color she had used for years. And then she got it in her head it was her turn to be the Lobster Queen. What did it matter, really, but she sulked about that one for the longest time. Just a lot of things combined to make her more distraught than she has ever been. Honestly, she hasn't been herself for quite a while."

So, Lester was not the only thing Delilah had that Patsy wanted for herself.

"Speaking of a drink, I could use one too," I said. "Mind if I join you girls?"

A little girl talk, I decided, might be just the thing.

CHAPTER SEVENTEEN

The next afternoon, Elizabeth walked in holding a flat box. "I have three photographs from the model boat competition of 1987," she announced with a big smile. "Plus a printed program and a news story too."

"Jackpot!" I said, excited. Just what Lisa Oldingham wanted most to find.

After Elizabeth set the box on her table, I gave her a high five. "And if it's possible, could you maybe…?"

"Sure," she said with a wink. "I'll call her right away and let her know the pieces could go quickly, with boating being such a big thing in the area and all."

Normally, I knew Elizabeth would hold materials for a week upon request, but time was of the essence.

The day seemed to fly by after that with lots of

orders going out, and a sale on paperbacks brought in a lot of eager readers. By the time I'd closed out the registers and locked up, I could really use that drink I'd scheduled with the ladies.

Thirty minutes after closing, the evening air felt perfect as I made my way to the High Tides bar on the south side of the beach. The place was doing a good business, but it wasn't hard to find the Divas I was meeting. Shards of light from the setting sun glinted like small spotlights off the diamond around Patsy's neck. And Judy's throaty laugh rose above the murmur of the growing crowd.

I gave them a little wave as I wove through the crowd, making my way to their table at the water's edge.

As I took my seat, Judy nodded at the mojito waiting at my place. A plastic shark was bobbing in the fancy glass beside a wedge of lime.

"House special," Judy said. "Two for the price of one, so I got one for you as well."

It occurred to me that having drinks with suspects in a poisoning case was not the smartest move—which really was a shame. I did love a mojito.

"Cheers." Patsy held up a Tequila Sunrise with a yellow duck floating in the glass. In a ruffled peasant blouse covered up with jewels, she seemed overdressed for a shorts and flip-flop kind of place, but if it made her happy, fine.

"I was telling Judy about that new man of mine," she told me with a wink. "Although we have yet to go public, and now he's going through...some things." She sighed, pausing for a sip. "But he says the sweetest things. I just have to share!"

Judy leaned back in her chair. "And I was telling Patsy romance is in the air. I have not yet revealed *my* news." She smiled. "But she and I, it seems, have a lot in common."

Oh, much more than they knew.

"Who says the young girls have a monopoly of love?" said Judy breezily. Then she lowered her voice. "Mine is also kind of private, for the moment anyway."

Hmm. They'd revealed the name to me, but they'd seemingly had second thoughts about how much they should say, at least to each other.

"Let's give hints!" said Judy

This could be interesting.

Or disastrous.

Longingly, I gazed at the mojito I probably shouldn't drink.

"Well, let's see," said Patsy, eager to play the game. "My man is a professional, a man of high intellect, as you might expect. Who gives me an exhilarating *dose* of romance in my life—if you get the hint."

A startled look crossed Judy's eyes. Then she took a breath before she spoke. "I'm proud to say *my* man is a beloved figure to many in this town. He does the best sort of work, because he is a healer."

Patsy's hand flew to her chest, and—whoops—I spilled my drink, making sure to aim it into the sand behind me and not on anybody's shoes. Especially not on Patsy's. The price tags on those heels might give me a heart attack.

"What a klutz I am," I cried, standing up. "Let me go replace this drink. Does anybody want something from the bar?"

Neither of them spoke as they stared, wide-eyed, at each other, and I sat back down. This was not the time to leave.

"Initial L?" asked Judy.

"Followed by an H?" asked Patsy.

They gasped in unison.

"How could you?" Patsy seethed after a startled silence.

"How could I do what?" asked Judy. "A nice man asked me out, and I said yes." She studied her friend across the table. "And then he asked me out again—and again. It's not much of a romance you have going, Patsy, if his eyes are elsewhere."

"Well, I could say the same for you." Patsy's face was white, and her hand was trembling as she reached for her drink. "He was supposed to drive me to the flower show last week before Delilah...well, you know."

They were silent for a while.

"Now, some things are making sense," Patsy said, crestfallen. "I do admit, things were moving kind of slow, but I just thought that at our age..." She hesitated for a moment. "And were you aware that Lester also had a little...something going with Delilah?"

Judy's mouth fell open, which we took as a "no."

"One of my customers mentioned to me she'd seen him quite a bit at dinner with Delilah—and one time at the opera—for Mozart's *Magic Flute,*" said Patsy. "I thought 'Surely not,' but then one night I went to see a show in Boston. And there they were, plain as day!" She stared down at the duck bobbing in her drink. "So now I have to wonder...how many of us could there be?"

The Magic Flute. Reg had said he'd heard a fight in Delilah's yard about a "magical bassoon." It must have been a flute instead!

With a hard look in her eye, Judy grabbed her drink. "He will have to make a choice," she told us firmly.

Patsy smoothed her hair behind her ear and met Judy's eye. "He will indeed," she said.

When the silence grew uncomfortable, Judy cleared her throat. "Or, on second thought, I think *we* should make a choice," she said to Patsy. "Because both of us deserve a man who will be honest with us." Then she glanced at me. "Rue, you need a drink." She stood. "Let me take care of that."

"I can get it. Thanks!" I was quick to say. Then I stood and made my way to the bar, which had gotten rather crowded.

When I returned with drinks for all, they had their heads together, whispering about the murder. Okay, that was good—since I had to somehow figure out if one of these unlikely suspects had done the unthinkable.

I stole a glance at Patsy as I handed her the drink. Reg had heard that fight between her and Delilah about *The Magic Flute.* And then I was pretty sure Patsy had returned to Delilah's place after her friend's death. I could not imagine why, but I had seen the evidence myself lying there among the flowers—those little paper words. Surely they were hers, as much as Patsy loved to show off her French. And I knew Delilah, proud gardener that she was, would have picked the trash up if she had been alive.

Judy broke through my reverie. "No matter what was

going on between Lester and Delilah," she told us in a solemn voice, "Delilah was my friend, and I will not rest easy until this thing is solved."

I took a sip—at last—of mojito. "I have heard," I whispered, "that she was being stalked in the days before the murder." I leaned in toward the Divas. "And that the stalker came back, wandering out in her yard, *after* she was killed."

Patsy scrunched her forehead as much as her Botox would allow. "Rue, what do you mean?" she asked.

"Oh, just rumors maybe." I took another sip. "But what I heard was this: There was an argument—out there in her yard—about ten days before she died. And Delilah for a while swore that there was someone creeping around her place." I paused. "But why would they come back *after* she was killed? To look for evidence, I guess?"

The drink in Judy's hand was shaking to the point I was afraid the little plastic shark would fly right off the rim.

Of course, neither of these women had a reason to tell me their secrets.

Unless I gave them one…

I waved a dismissive hand. "But these kinds of things, I guess, are not for us to ponder. Because I'm pretty sure the cops know exactly who has come and gone from Delilah's place."

Patsy almost choked on her Tequila Sunrise.

"Delilah, I can bet, had all kinds of security set up," I explained. (And maybe it was true.) "Cameras and all of that, as frightened as she was of every little thing. So I'm pretty sure the cops were watching all the action in her yard."

"This isn't good," said Patsy, breathing hard.

"I was there—in the yard!" whispered Judy. "I was there more than once, not long after she was killed. And before as well. But I swear I had my reasons."

Patsy hesitated. "You're not the only one," she said. She lightly touched her friend's hand. "I'll tell if you go first."

CHAPTER EIGHTEEN

"It was nothing!" Judy said. "It was just to catch a kitten, the sweetest little thing. And it was important; I was handling the last thing Delilah asked of me. But now I know it might look awful—really, really bad." She stared down into her drink. "She'd let me know, you see, that there was a stray I should come and get in her neighborhood." A softness filled her eyes. "And you know how Delilah was. It just broke her heart how forlorn the poor thing looked. She would give him food if he showed up at her house, but then he would dash off and stay gone for days." She paused. "Delilah couldn't bear to think of that poor baby out there on his own. She wanted him to have a home."

"Delilah was a softie," I said with a nod.

"She wasn't even mad that this little guy had made a

mess out in her garden, digging like he did," said Judy. "We put out some grapefruit peels to try to keep him away from the flowers, like I do with my plants. Cats hate the smell of citrus." Then her eyes grew wide and she grabbed my arm. "Once when I was there, somebody else showed up, somebody with a dog. I think it was a cop; they do use dogs, you know, at least on the TV. I thought my running days were over, but I got out of there real fast. It was a close call."

Patsy stared at her. "Why on earth, Judy, would you run? No one would think a thing about you being in the yard to try and catch a cat."

Judy slowly twirled her glass. "Let's just say that in my younger days, I was a little wild. It was just my instinct, I suppose, not to want the cops to find me in the yard of their latest murder victim." She held up a hand as if to dispel whatever criminal scenarios might have popped into our heads. "I was never all that bad," she said. "I just hung out with a crowd who didn't let some useless rules get in the way of our good time. Like, there was this one night in my early twenties when we stole a van from some senior center. It was after midnight, way past these people's bedtimes, so what could it hurt?"

Judy's lips tugged up into a smile. "What a night that was!" she said. "We took that thing for a spin all the way into Boston, partied at some clubs, and brought it back all safe and sound before the place had even opened. No one would have known except some cops were on patrol right when we brought it back. How is that for some bad luck?"

"Hmph." Patsy brushed a strand of glossy hair out of her eye. "I don't see Lester getting serious with someone with *a record*."

Judy flashed her friend a look as she picked up her mojito. "And now there is something else that has me freaking out," she said, leaning closer to us. "The cops, I understand, have been asking lots of questions about this stupid berry drink that Constance insisted I start serving. Because the rumor is the killer slipped a little something into one of my Berry Blasts, and that's what killed Delilah!"

"No!" Patsy's hand flew up to her mouth.

"So I hid it from the menu!" Judy whispered. Her mouth was set in a firm line. "But if it *was* used in the murder—and they figured out the drink came from my café—how bad would that look? For the cops to see some tape of me out wandering in Delilah's yard?" Then she turned to Judy. "Enough of my sad story. What's the deal with you?"

Patsy sighed. "This doesn't make me look good, and I'm actually ashamed. I wasn't at my best when I figured out the truth about Lester and Delilah. I wish I'd let myself calm down just a little before marching over to her house, but I was furious—and hurt." She paused to take a sip of her tequila. "Delilah was outside, as she often was, working in her garden late, and I said some things I wish I could take back. Almost instantly, I knew that I'd gone too far. And now Delilah's gone."

When Patsy's voice broke with that last sentence, Judy touched her hand. "Don't beat yourself up about it," she told Patsy softly. "All of us have our moments."

"After that, I tried to make things right with her," continued Patsy. "Oh, I was still upset—because Lester was *my* man—but I knew I'd been too harsh. So I made her some cupcakes to tell her I was sorry." Patsy rolled her eyes. "What was I even thinking? Nothing that I ever cook turns out halfway decent, even though they did look lovely."

"It's the thought that counts," I said.

"That might have done the trick," said Patsy, "but I was still so hurt and not on my best behavior. There were still some times I was rather frosty with her." She let out a sigh. "But she'd been my friend forever, and I thought if I was friendly, she might back away from Lester. Toward the end, we'd planned a lunch, but then Delilah died before we could go." Patsy shook her head. "She was just so sweet to me despite the way I acted.

Even told me to stop by and pick some flowers from her garden anytime I liked. She had lavender this year, which she knew I loved. So I stopped by her place after she died to take some of that. And I spent a little time out there on her bench, practicing my French—which is, as you might know, *le langage de l'amour!* I'm taking a new course."

I thought about what they'd told me as I finished up my drink. "Oh!" I looked up at Judy. "Did you ever catch the cat?"

"I did, a few days later. It was the spotted cat you were asking me about when you came in yesterday." She sighed. "Most cats do okay at the café for long stretches, but that one loves to cuddle, and I can tell he really wants to find his person soon."

"Cute name," Patsy said.

"He's a fan of pie, it seems," said Judy with a smile. "One of the neighbors told me he came to her house one night—with a lot of crumbs and blueberry bits all stuck up in his whiskers." She laughed. "Someone on the street, I guess, went without dessert that night."

We all shared a smile, and I leaned back in my chair, inclined to believe their stories—which meant that fewer questions were swirling through my mind. But there still was the matter of Theodore Oldingham—and possibly a financial motive for Delilah's death.

"Not to bring up a sore subject," I began, "but do you ladies think Lester is okay? You know, with the business? Things haven't seemed so busy the last few times I've been in."

"That worries me a lot," Judy told me with a nod. "He's seemed distracted lately, and one night when we were out to dinner, there was this man across the room who kept giving us the eye. I could tell that Lester was trying very hard to avoid this guy. I knew who he was because he comes into the café every now and then. He sells medical equipment, and I had to wonder if Lester owed him money."

"One thing that I've noticed," said Patsy thoughtfully, "is that he doesn't like to spend as freely as he used to when we started going out. We'd go to half-price movies. Or just walk on the beach."

Dating three (or more?) women could get pricey, especially for a man whose business was in trouble.

"And someone, I'm pretty sure, was putting pressure on the poor man," Judy said. "I heard him on the phone once, and things started getting heated. He was insisting to this person that it was not their place to tell him how to run his business. That their job was to support and not to dictate what he did."

Hmm. I had a good idea who might be pressuring the doctor. Every business person in our town had entertained that thought about Constance at one time or another: it was her job as head of guild to help the merchants and not to make demands about how we operated.

"Did he get more specific?" I leaned in to Judy.

She thought about it for a moment. "All I know is that this person wanted him to do some specific thing. Like, it maybe had to do with how he set his prices, who he had working for him. You know, that sort of thing."

Who he had working for him! I could just imagine Constance pushing Lester to let Delilah go. That day in his office she had made no secret of her disdain for Delilah.

What I didn't understand was why he would give in.

CHAPTER NINETEEN

*T*he next day as I shelved some books, a scene played over in my head: Constance berating poor Delilah as she handed her that drink. What was it that she'd said?

"Something about paying more attention," I mumbled to myself. "And how a mistake one day could send a patient to the grave."

"To the grave!" the parrot repeated loudly, startling a customer who was browsing in the science fiction section.

Stacey passed with an armload of books and giggled. "Zeke keeps things interesting," she said.

"One mistake!" Zeke called.

I met Stacey's eye and laughed. "It's never boring with the pets," I said. "How's it going, Stacey?"

"Well, I was working earlier today at An Elegant Bouquet, which meant time with Constance. But there's good news—I escaped!"

What a coincidence, given the fact that Constance had been on my mind. "What did our friend have you doing?" I asked Stacey.

"Oh, just the usual—sprucing up the place before she opened for the day," said Stacey, setting down the stack of books. "It was kind of a sad morning, if you want to know the truth."

"How come?"

"Oh, just something that I saw," she said, leaning against a shelf. "Normally, of course, I just pick up the piles of paper, dust beneath those things, and move along. They're none of my business, really, and kind of boring, I'd imagine. But today this paper fell out of a file, and I saw Delilah's name." She paused. "It was on a torn-out page from one of those to-do pads Constance always buys—with 'From the Desk of Constance Asher' printed out across the top. She always dates those things, and this page was kind of old, from about four months ago." Stacey touched my hand and gave me a sad look. "It was a reminder, Rue, to cancel flowers someone ordered for Delilah's birthday. With a note that said 'deceased.' It was a standing order, I believe. Delilah got those flowers every year. It just made me so sad, that little piece of paper in that file, anchored down by a begonia so it wouldn't blow away."

From Lester I imagined. He seemed to like sending flowers.

Then my stomach dropped. "Wait a minute, Stacey. Did you say four months ago?"

"Yeah, it had been there a while, I guess," she said.

"Then how did Constance know that—"

Stacey gasped as her hand flew to her mouth.

"You should tell the cops," I said.

She nodded, her face white. "Let me make a call," she said.

My heart was beating rapidly as I continued shelving books. My thoughts were running wild as I heard a shuffling behind me and turned toward the sound.

"Oh, excuse me," said a dark-haired woman, smoothing down the skirt of her business suit. "Could you tell me, please, where I could find Elizabeth?"

I gave her a smile. "Let me go and find her. She must be in the back."

"Tell her my name is Lisa; she'd called about some photos she found for me to see."

Theodore's daughter had arrived, it seemed.

"I'm Rue, by the way," I said. "Welcome to the Seabreeze. I will be right back."

"Welcome to the Seabreeze!" repeated Zeke, who was certainly talkative today.

Lisa's eyes grew wide in surprise, then she let out a loud laugh. "Well, that's a friendly bird," she said.

As I passed Elizabeth's table on my way to the back room, I quietly rearranged a line of photos, pulling the one of Constance and Theodore toward the front, hoping it might draw a comment from our guest. Perhaps one more of the mysteries would soon be solved, and we would find out how—and if—Theodore Oldingham was connected to the case.

And with the suspicious note Stacey had discovered, an arrest might be coming any minute.

I passed Stacey in an aisle after I'd told Elizabeth that her guest had arrived.

Stacey gave me a nervous smile. "I did it," she reported. "I told them I had information, and the lady told me someone would call me back."

I helped a customer find a new release and chatted with her about the author, a favorite of mine as well. After I rang up her purchase, I wandered to the table where Elizabeth and Lisa were excitedly looking over my best friend's recent finds.

"My father loved this stuff," said Lisa, "and I can't believe you got your hands on something this specific and this old. I can't wait to show my children. Because when they were young, he got them involved with his love for model boats. This was absolutely worth the drive from Yarmouth!"

"And if your father's still around," I said, playing dumb, "what lovely memories this will be for him."

Her smile dimmed a little. "I'm afraid we lost him, and that's been hard for all of us. Which is why I've sent myself on this little quest to…try to find out more about the things he loved."

"I'm so sorry," I told her.

"I appreciate it." She frowned and breathed in deeply. "Now, let's talk about something fun, like this program here." She picked up the program from the decades-old model boating competition. "It still stings a little to talk about my father's passing," she said quietly.

And that is when she noticed the photograph of him and Constance.

Her hand went to her mouth. "What in the world?" she exclaimed. "That's my father in the picture!"

Elizabeth explained she'd pulled the picture for a display about best friends. "Of course, I don't know your father," said Elizabeth, "but when I came across this photo at a sale, I recognized Constance Asher, who's head of our merchants guild in town."

"Oh, yes. She and Dad were close." Lisa seemed to be near tears. "I think this is a sign, that he's here with me today. That he likes what I am doing—finding things to give my kids about these little boats that became their hobby."

"Do you know, I believe that you are right," Elizabeth told her gently.

"Constance tried to help us after my father died," said Lisa. "She was as mad as we were about what happened to him. He didn't have to die! And Constance tried to make sure that someone paid for what they had done. So another family wouldn't have to suffer like we did."

I put a hand on her back. "Oh, my goodness, Lisa. What happened to your father?"

"Oh, it's a long, sad story. And that is in the past." She picked up the photo. "But how happy he looks here!"

"Mistake! Mistake!" called Zeke. "Send a patient to the grave!"

All the color drained from Lisa's face when she heard the parrot's words. "How did that bird know?" she asked. Then she took a breath. "My father was a patient," she explained, "and a series of mistakes—inexcusable mistakes—caused him to lose his life." She paused, breathing hard before she continued. "Some ditz at the doctor's office got a message all mixed up so that he didn't get the meds he absolutely had to have. And when he called in with some symptoms—and should have seen the doctor—the doctor never even knew that my father called."

My heart seized up. "Do you know the woman's name?" I asked. "From the doctor's office?"

"We tried to find out, but we couldn't," Lisa told us with a sigh. "And shortly after that, she took another job and moved away. I decided with my brother we would not pursue it. It wouldn't bring our father back, and we wanted to move on. But Constance always told us she would do her best to somehow find the woman."

And something told me that she had.

After Lisa left the store with her treasures, I went to the back counter, where Stacey was preparing orders to go out. "Any word from the police?"

"Still waiting for that call," she said.

"Do you happen to know where Delilah worked before she worked for Lester?" I asked her.

She thought about it for a minute. "I could be mistaken, but I believe she moved from Yarmouth."

"I'll be back," I said. "I believe I need some air."

I grabbed the leash and called for Gatsby, and we strolled through the town while I processed the new information. Before long, I found myself staring at the entrance to An Elegant Bouquet.

I pulled out my phone, and this time Andy answered. "Pack your fishing poles," I said. "You're about to make an arrest, and your vacation can begin."

CHAPTER TWENTY

onstance emerged from the store with a delivery just as Andy jogged up, looking out of sorts. "Oh, Rue, there you are. Perhaps we should discuss—"

I crossed my arms as Constance nodded and tried to hurry past us with a bouquet of pink roses, carnations, and calla lilies.

"How dare you!" I told her. "First you pressure Lester to tell Delilah that she's fired, but that is not enough. You have to take her life."

She momentarily looked startled but soon gained her composure. "That's preposterous," she said, "and you're standing in my way. I have business to conduct."

"Your friend Theodore—you did it all for him," I said.

"Wait! You were acquainted with Theodore Olding-ham?" Andy said to Constance.

"Rue, how did you..." She soon recovered from her shock. "That is just absurd. Please move."

"The two of them were best friends," I explained to Andy.

"Interesting," he murmured, almost to himself. "I had a hunch the murder and his death might somehow be connected."

"I demand you let me pass!" barked Constance. "Having a best friend is not against the law."

"No, but murder is," I said. "And no one but the killer would have canceled a delivery scheduled for Delilah months before her death."

"Do you have evidence of that?" asked Andy.

I believe you will find the note in a folder on the top of a filing cabinet in her office, anchored down by a begonia," I said calmly. "It's written on a list with her name and a date across the top."

"You are nothing but a no-good meddler!" Constance jabbed a finger in my face. "Did you ever stop to think that Delilah's death could have *saved* some lives?"

"Are you confessing?" Andy asked her, moving closer.

"I am doing no such thing!" she said defiantly.

"So you wouldn't mind if I take a look there in your office?" Andy asked, tilting his head to study Constance.

"Do you have a warrant?" she asked, shifting her flowers to her other arm.

"I could get one soon—or you could save us both some time," he told her sternly.

"Suit yourself," she said with a sigh, sinking down onto a bench behind her. "What a foolish world we live in. Inefficiency, it seems, makes you beloved in this town. Wins you votes for the pathetic title of Somerset Harbor Lobster Queen! But to step in boldly to remove a menace from our midst? I'm afraid what that will get you is a pair of handcuffs. Like a common criminal."

As I drove Andy to the airport three days later, he was full of updates. Constance, he reported, was telling all the jailers how to do their job.

"No surprise." I laughed.

Andy shook his head. "They warn me every day not to bring in another one like her, or they'll run me out of town."

She had confessed right there on the sidewalk, smart enough to understand the gig was up. Later at the station, the whole story had come out.

It was during her lunches with Delilah to discuss

their science books that Constance had come to understand the connection Delilah had with Theodore. They were discussing their past jobs when Delilah dropped the name of the doctor she had worked with before.

That's when Constance started her campaign to have Delilah fired. And her anger only grew when votes poured in for Delilah to become the Lobster Queen. After venting her anger in the note, Constance had fixed the vote so the crown had gone instead to Ellen Cason.

Soon, it was not enough that Delilah lose her job. Constance was afraid she'd only go to work for another doctor and still endanger lives. And thus began the slow poisoning of Delilah.

At first, Constance would drop off "treats" at Lester's office, handing a "special" cookie to Delilah and making sure she ate it so nobody else would suffer by mistake. Then she picked Delilah to assist with the bingo game so she'd have an excuse to have meals out with her victim and slip a little something extra in her food. And, of course, there was that drink.

"What she put Lester through!" I said as we neared the airport.

Andy shook his head. "Lester and the ladies!"

One of Andy's jobs as the cops wrapped up the case had been a final interview with Lester. Apparently the doctor had been clueless that the ladies would assign romantic motives to his invitations to go out—not to mention the bouquets he sent on their birthdays. As a longtime physician, Lester had observed the way depression and ill health could set in as a result of being lonely. And the good doctor had decided nights out on the town might be the perfect thing to stave off depression for his single patients. Plus, it was company for him.

"Did you know that loneliness can, in fact, reshape the brain?" asked Andy, wiping a crumb of his breakfast muffin from his shirt. "That's what Lester said."

When it became apparent that Lester had left several ladies with the wrong idea, the poor guy had been flustered. "A brilliant man of science and absolutely clueless in the ways women's minds can work," said Andy.

Things had hit him all at once: financial worries, women trouble, and the need to fire Delilah, which had been devastating for the kind-hearted doctor. "Some of the creditors got really ugly with Delilah when they would call into the office," Andy said. "So we had to look at some of them to see if this business with finances might have played a role in what happened to her."

Constance had threatened Lester that if he didn't fire Delilah, she'd expose Delilah's role in the death of her friend. And Lester would do anything to keep Delilah from the knowledge that a man had died because of what she liked to call her "whoopsie moments."

"Well, enough about work," said Andy. "How did the podcast go?"

"It went great," I said. Which had been a relief. Now I'd have more time for yoga with the goats, which was really helping me to feel less tense.

Andy frowned and rubbed his head as he gazed out the window.

"You okay?" I asked.

"You know, I'm still not sure this is the best time for me to be heading out of town," he said.

"You have earned this, Andy," I assured him. "And Blueberry's in good hands. I do know a thing or two when it comes to cats."

After the arrest, Andy had spent some time at Judy's, getting a statement from her about the Berry Blast. And that is when the smallest kitten in the café at last picked out her human.

"Gatsby, Beasley, and Ollie will keep him entertained while you're off catching fish," I reassured him.

Andy frowned, unsure, being brand new to the business of caring for a pet. He had always claimed he was much too busy to take on a new member of his household. But, as Judy always said, the cats do the choosing—and the cats are never wrong. I'd never seen Andy more content than when the little kitten was snuggled in his lap. Blueberry had chosen well.

"He won't feel abandoned?" he asked now, the crease deepening in his brow as I pulled into the airport.

"When I left this morning, he was snuggled in a heap with my two. All of them were tired from chasing Ollie's favorite toy across the floor." Gatsby had been keeping a loving watch over the newcomer as she snoozed.

As I pulled up to the curb, Andy got out of the car and pulled his bags out of the back, finally convinced.

I lifted my hand in a wave. "Now, go and catch some fish."

# # #

Thank you for reading! Want to help out?

Reviews are crucial for independent authors like me, so if you enjoyed my book, **please consider leaving a review today**.

Thank you!

Penny Brooke

ABOUT THE AUTHOR

Penny Brooke has been reading mysteries for as long as she can remember. When not penning her own stories, she enjoys spending time outdoors with her husband, crocheting, and cozying up with her pups and a good novel. To find out more about her books, visit www.pennybrooke.com

Made in United States
Orlando, FL
21 July 2024

49350330R00088